Nick Tyrone is a writer and political commentator who has written for the *New Statesman*, *Daily Telegraph*, *Independent* and *Daily Express*. He has also appeared on *BBC News*, *Good Morning Britain*, *Sky News*, *Al Jeezera* and *Intelligence Squared*. In 2017, he wrote the book *Apocalypse Delayed: Why the Left is Still in Trouble* about the future of UK politics.

Nick lives in London with his family. *Dead Idol* is his debut novel.

www.nicktyrone.com
 @NicholasTyrone

G000242804

DEAD IDOL

NICK TYRONE

ACCENT

The right of Nick Tyrone to be identified as the Author of
the Work has been asserted by him in accordance with the
Copyright, Designs and Patents Act 1988.

First published in 2019 as *Pop Star Jihadi* by Radix

First published in this edition in 2020 by
HEADLINE PUBLISHING GROUP

1

Cataloguing in Publication Data is available from the British Library

ISBN 978 1 7861 5780 5

Typeset in 10.5/13.75pt Bembo Std by Jouve (UK), Milton Keynes

Printed and bound in Great Britain by Clays Ltd, Elcograf S.p.A.

Headline's policy is to use papers that are natural, renewable and recyclable
products and made from wood grown in well-managed forests and other
controlled sources. The logging and manufacturing processes are expected
to conform to the environmental regulations of the country of origin.

HEADLINE PUBLISHING GROUP
An Hachette UK Company
Carmelite House
50 Victoria Embankment
London
EC4Y 0DZ

www.headline.co.uk
www.hachette.co.uk

To my wife, Polly

'A new, dark decade has begun', by David O'Willery, *New York Express* commentary section, June 17th, 2021

Last night, the twenties began.

As I got into a cab to take me to Madison Square Garden, less than an hour after the bomb had gone off, the details were still hazy. Snippets of news reached me in episodic flashes. Each text from a colleague left me ever more eager to get downtown. The only concrete facts I had was that a bomb had gone off at Madison Square Garden and some of those in attendance at a concert there had been killed. The number of casualties was unclear at that stage.

Arrival in front of the Garden brought with it immediately the full, unfathomable tragedy of what had taken place that evening, a feeling I was wholly unprepared for. Opaque blankets of smoke still billowed forth from the building as an army of firemen ran to and fro. I witnessed a herd of paramedics entering and exiting the arena, the ones coming in wheeling empty stretchers. The ones coming out again had those same stretchers occupied. Every stretcher leaving the scene bore a sheet fully covering the body it carried.

At one point I saw a little girl, perhaps eleven or twelve years of age, swaddled in bandages. She was crying hysterically as medical professionals carried her from the arena. I couldn't understand why she wasn't on a stretcher – until I reasoned that there were only enough on hand to service the deceased, so great was their number.

Speaking to other journalists gathered in front of the site brought me up to speed. It had been a Noah Hastings concert. A bomb had gone off early on in the show. Death toll was at least fifty. Most of the dead were under eighteen years of age. Then came the real news: Hastings himself had been killed in the blast.

At least, that was what we thought was the real news at the time.

About an hour on from when I had first arrived at the smoldering MSG, word travelled around the assembled press corps that Noah Hastings had been attached to the bomb itself and was likely to have been the one who had detonated it. This was confirmed in age-old fashion: the police wouldn't comment on any questions about Hastings as the assailant. It appeared that one of the biggest pop stars in the world had just committed a suicide bombing, in the middle of Manhattan, murdering a cabal of his most devoted fans along the way.

Eventually, there was a small press conference at which the police confirmed at least this much to us, as well as that the death toll had been confirmed at ninety-two, with several victims not yet identified. That number included, of course, Noah Hastings himself. As the press conference concluded, most of the hacks went home or to the office, determined to escape from the Stygian aftermath of the incident still being swept away. I decided to stick around and see if I could interview a few survivors.

'At this moment in time, I'm choosing to believe that it didn't happen,' said one girl who was on the balcony during the concert. She was not injured in the blast save for what has been diagnosed as a temporary case of tinnitus. 'I mean, obviously it happened – I was there, I saw the explosion – but I don't think it happened the way you guys are saying it did.'

The 'you guys' reference let me know that this was not this girl of fifteen's first interview that evening. She was wearing a 'Noah Hastings for President' T-shirt. I pressed her on what she had meant by her last sentence.

'I don't think that was really Noah up there tonight. He sounded different, less good than normal. I think that was a stunt double or something up there. No one really died, that's what I think. It was all just staged so that Noah would look bad. The whole front of the arena was obviously stuffed with crash test dummies or something, I remember that much.'

I managed to interview a handful of other kids who had been in the Gardens when the bomb had gone off. Most of them had a similarly offbeat take to that of my initial interviewee that night.

'It was a CIA thing – they wanted Noah to go undercover in China and needed to fake his death.'

Noah Hastings is the most famous westerner in China. That includes the President of the United States. He couldn't have walked five feet anywhere in that country without being recognized by people.

'Noah has a stunt double. He was used in *Monkey Trouble*. Noah wanted to drop out of society, so he hired that guy to take a bomb for him.'

Monkey Trouble was the not wholly successful attempt to translate Noah Hastings' pop stardom onto the big screen. Its plot revolves around a lower primate pet of Noah's escaping from his Los Angeles mansion and trying to walk across that city. In the movie, Noah tries to trace the monkey's path and bring it back into the fold while stopping here and there to sing a song or two. It is an unholy mixture of *Bonzo Goes to College*, *Singin' in the Rain* and *Falling Down* that takes on whole new levels of offensiveness after the events of last night. At one point in the film, Hastings makes a joke about suicide bombers that was in bad taste at the time, never mind now.

It is not a good idea to take the opinions of a group of teenagers who have been witness to a bombing at close quarters as being reflective of society as a whole and how it will react to the events of yesterday evening. Yet if social media this morning has anything to say about it, it is precisely that the things I heard outside of Madison Square Garden last night are being echoed amongst the wider populace. As expected, the automatic connection between a suicide bombing having taken place and Islam being involved in some way runs very deep in the American psyche. Theories like this have been widely disseminated online already. I thought about quoting some of them. I refrained once I realized all of them were unprintable for one reason or another.

This is why I will say again that the twenties have now begun. 'Hastings Wednesday' ended one epoch and begat another. It arrives right at the moment we had started to feel safe in the knowledge that America itself was largely to be free of the kind of terrorist activity seen in Europe over the last several years. Shattered by the act of a young man from the deep south of this country committing suicide with a bomb strapped to his chest, killing almost a hundred children in the heart of New York City. As we scramble around for answers in the coming weeks as to why this horrific event took place, some will fill in the blanks with whatever comes easiest to hand. Be that Zionist conspiracy theories, suicidal stunt doubles, or sadly if so, the hand of international Islamist-inspired terrorism, let us be under no illusion that this is simply more of what we have seen before. We are entering a new age, one considerably unlike any that humanity has experienced in the recent past. For how will the newly christened Generation Hastings cope once the conspiracy theories have proven poor comfort? And if we can't be safe from someone like Noah Hastings, from whom can we be safe? In this nascent era, which began last night, the answer is clear: no one at all.

A small advert in the *New York Sentinel*, June 18th, 2021

We the bereaved, each one of us having had one or more of our children's lives ended tragically prematurely by the unfortunate incident at Madison Square Garden on Wednesday evening, are making several pleas to the general public.

Most of us have had the death of our beloved child or children tragically confirmed. Still others amongst our number have children who were at the concert and have been missing since, but these parents remain living in hope. On the page facing this advert are pictures of several children from the concert last night who have yet to be found. If you have any information on the whereabouts of any of them, please call the number given below.

We also ask that the hatred, online and elsewhere, cease immediately. We have no idea why a pop star would do what Noah Hastings did. We may well never know. At least until the facts are better known, could we all calm down and stop throwing around conspiracy theories? Particularly given some of these theories have been directed at us. Several of our number have had to face hateful messages on social media – some of them saying that our children are not actually dead and that we must therefore be involved in some sort of conspiracy. Please be assured that none of us are involved in any conspiracy to obscure the truth. Our children have been torn away from us. That we are suffering the loss of our loved ones is terrible enough without having to carry the added burden of such hateful things being thrown in our direction.

Finally, as part of this plea, could everyone stop targeting one particular creed or religion for what took place, please? We have no evidence that Noah Hastings acted under the influence of anything other than his own callousness. Again, it only makes the horrible suffering all of us are experiencing at the moment worse to know that our deceased children are being used as pawns in some sort of ideological warfare.

We make these three pleas to everyone in not only the tri-state area but the whole of America, in particular those who have children of their own. Children who are still alive; kids who still have a future, unlike ours. Please, put yourself in our position and imagine the horror. Then picture how much easier it would be if everyone listened to what we needed in our most desperate hour. In most of our cases, we have lost everything that was precious to us. Please, let your prayers be with us and our children who have departed at this time, and not with those who would wish to cause trouble out of this tragic incident.

Signed,
The parents of the Ninety-One

'It's Islam, dummy', a piece by blogger Joyce Randall, June 20th, 2021

Holy shit, right? What we've been thinking was a ripe possibility for many a year now has finally dropped, yo. Noah Hastings straps on a bomb before a concert, trots out onto the stage, and then blows himself and ninety-one fans (and possibly counting – there are seven children still unaccounted for, although there are also several bodies yet to be identified) to smithereens. I've been saying for years that radical Islam was someday soon going to infiltrate white, Christian culture – but even I didn't think Noah Hastings, the most cornball, white bread douchebag on planet Earth, would be the one to light the fuse. In retrospect, I should have known.

The signs were always there. Hastings was part of the liberal, Trump-hating elite that always saw Islam not only as something totally compatible with the American way of life, but as something *essential* to that way of life as they reconstructed it. A group of people for whom the Islamification of America was both something that wasn't going to happen – in fact, was a figment of the fevered imaginations of right-wing pundits such as I – and yet also something to be welcomed, even if by some chance it wasn't simply the delusions of the Trump-friendly. Hastings was part of a Hollywood clique that sees any criticism of Islam whatsoever as 'racism'. It was only a matter of time before one of them went full towel-head, strapped a bomb to their chest and slaughtered a pile of innocents.

As horrible as the deaths of ninety-one kids undoubtedly is, we need to start seeing the upside in all of this. After the Noah Hastings suicide, no one can tell us that Islam isn't piercing its way into the very soul of American life, corrupting its very beating heart. We're no longer talking about Saudi immigrants as suicide bombers here, but a kid from Louisiana raised Baptist. If Noah Hastings can go Bin Laden on us, anyone can.

So, what should we do now? The most important thing is to not allow the liberal MSM to establish their warped version of the story as the one of historical record. There will be a battle for hearts and minds over the next few weeks and we need to be the ones who come out of it the victors. You all know as well as I do that any chance they get will see the liberal establishment attempt to deflect the blame away from Islam and onto something else. The New York State Police, the FBI, the CIA, all of them will be in on this. We need to call them all out at every turn and remind people that no one, particularly a redneck kid from the deep south whose father was a preacher, blows themselves up for no reason whatsoever. The only thing that could have caused someone to commit such an act was a deep-seated belief in the tenets of the Muslim faith — what other religion is currently driving its adherents to such barbarity? When was the last time you heard about the Buddhist threat stalking the land? Or about how a horde of Shintoists were planning to blow up a federal building?

We need to say this and say this again and again until it gets through to the American public. Or at least, the portion of the American public which still retains an open mind; those who haven't been poisoned irreparably by liberal politics; those who can still be reached by reason.

Almost certainly for the time being, only those of us on the supposed 'alt-right' will be the ones saying any of what I've just said, political correctness keeping everyone else's tongues at bay. That only puts more of the onus on each and every one of us to shout as loudly as we can. It may get unpleasant over the coming weeks. Yet we cannot fail in our mission, Christian soldiers. Our time is now. If the rise of pop-star jihadis is on the menu, it's time to burn the restaurant down.

'I was meant to be there', by James Hillel. article in the *New York Sentinel*, June 20th, 2021,

As the lead popular culture journalist on this newspaper, it was my unwanted job to sit through two hours of Noah Hastings music at Madison Square Garden and then write about what I'd heard. I dreaded it like you would not believe for a week beforehand. I am exposed to a lot of music I do not like in my job, but none as vapid and tuneless as the Hastings 'songbook'. He always sounded to me like a man deep within the pains of a large bowel movement that wouldn't budge as he huffed and puffed his way through his panoply of horrible tunes, the unbearable synth pads that accompanied him something out of a Bananarama-inspired, 1980s-inflected nightmare.

I tried everything I could to get out of the job; no one wanted to take my place, even for the lure of some of the delightful favours I am able to bestow by virtue of my position. I promised one guy who covers grassroots New York stuff a month's worth of Mets tickets I had managed to get by trading in very nice seats at the opera. He didn't even need to think about it before giving me a solid, unmistakable no. For context, this is a guy with the names of the starting XI Mets 1986 team tattooed on his back, so I'm clearly not the only journalist in this town with a deep-seated aversion to Noah Hastings.

It looked like I was stuck with the gig – until fate intervened, at least. I awoke on the morning of June 16th with a very sick child on my hands. When I went to rouse her, my daughter Eli complained that her side hurt. My heart started to race; as a parent, you learn to differentiate between your children's phony complaints to get attention and when they are actually ill. This was definitely in the latter camp. She looked like she was running a fever, so I took her temperature. One hundred and four. Her lips and fingertips were blue and she was slipping in and out of consciousness. In a panic, I wrapped her up in a blanket (why is this our first instinct with children who are burning up from the inside?) and almost literally threw her into my '02 Dodge Romero. I then burnt rubber getting to Mount Sinai Emergency. She was checked in quickly (thank God) and I was left alone to stew.

I was sitting there in the waiting room for a long time, my thoughts entirely preoccupied by my daughter's health as you would expect. My phone ringing brought me back to the real world. It was my wife. I'd tried calling her earlier, only to get her voicemail, so I'd texted her what had happened.

'What took you so long to get back to me?' was how I opened the conversation, not terribly warmly. I was stunned that it had taken her over an hour to respond to a desperate text, telling her that her daughter was on the brink of death.

'Sorry, I was having a nap after a meeting. Jet lag.'

My wife was on a business trip in Europe. I instantly felt bad that I'd been so rude.

'I'm sorry. Just worried.'

'How is she?'

'No word yet.'

It then kicked in that with my daughter sick and my wife out of the country, I faced a dilemma, one that wasn't altogether unpleasant in the current context. I could use the whole set-up of my ill child as a pretext to get out of the Noah Hastings concert/article deal. And it wouldn't involve the slightest hint of deception whatsoever.

There were problems with this course of action despite its transparency. One, I had been less than secretive in terms of my desire to pass the buck at work on this score, what with attempting to bribe most of my colleagues into taking the gig for me; the Noah Hastings dartboard I had erected in my cubicle wasn't helpful. The timing would be questioned by my editor, straight off. But my daughter was sick, something the hospital trip proved beyond any doubt, so there was a comeback there. The second thing to consider was whether I was using my daughter's condition unfairly, a moral question arising from it all, in other words. But no – someone had to be at the hospital until she was discharged or at least there was more information available. I called work and told the Big Cheese about the situation. He was so unconvinced at first that I had to get the Emergency Ward receptionist to confirm that I was indeed at the hospital.

'I suppose you're now going to say I got some random woman to pose as a hospital receptionist, right?' I asked him after having taken the phone back.

'No, that was a bona fide receptionist all right. Some things in this world can't be faked. You're off the hook, Hillel. I'll get Jefferson to cover it.'

About half an hour later, I was told that my daughter had been unconscious for a while and they had her on a drip while they did some tests. She was going to be fine, they told me, the words frozen in mid-air as they were spoken. She just had a terrible flu, thank all the gods that might or might not exist in the universe. The pain in the side was an odd symptom that showed up in about one in ten children with this particular flu strain. They wanted to keep her in overnight. I was told in no uncertain terms that I should go home and come back in the morning to see her, particularly as they were giving her a sedative. It occurred to me at this point that if I hurried I could just about catch the start of the Noah Hastings concert. This prompted the first chuckle from me of the day.

I left Mount Sinai and drove back to my apartment downtown feeling relieved beyond description. I parked the car in my building's lot and remembered we needed food. I was walking down to the local Wholefoods when I heard the explosion. Hearing it from almost fifty blocks away, it sounded like it could have been any number of things. Possibly a large fireworks display, but the sound of it was too close for the visuals to have been out of range (the Wholefoods in question having a glass roof, for context). I couldn't think of what else it could be, so I put it out of mind and got on with buying my falafels. You see and hear a lot of weird stuff in New York City, and if you dwelt on every odd occurrence, you'd soon become deranged.

When I got home, I turned on the news, which was of course covered with the Hastings bombing already. When what happened first hit me, I panicked like you would not believe, almost losing control of my bodily functions. My reaction was one you'd expect if I'd found out a plane I had a ticket for but arrived late to the airport to catch had been blown up in mid-air. I suppose in many respects the two situations are not all that far removed from one another, at least in the essentials. I quickly calmed down as I realized the unlikelihood of having been in harm's way even if I'd been present at the Garden that evening. The press box was completely unaffected, with no injuries whatsoever, something a few phone calls confirmed for me (the first being to Jefferson himself, my cover, who was completely fine). Even so, I couldn't shake off the feeling that I'd just escaped death through some sort of miracle.

As a result of this mortal panic and guilt about the possibility of having sent poor Jefferson to the slaughter (he's not yet thirty and has three kids, just to add to my feelings of self-reproach until I had managed to get a hold of him), it took me almost an hour after I'd heard about the bombing to grasp the full absurdity of it all. A pop star in his mid-twenties had blown himself up (even the initial speculation that we were fed in the immediate aftermath of the explosion seemed to point to his direct involvement in the bombing itself, if you remember), taking a contingent of his fans with him. The ones in the front rows, the kids who had almost certainly camped out for several nights consecutively to secure the tickets, all to see the young man they loved and trusted above possibly anyone else in the world. And Hastings had slaughtered them, literally. Given how much I loathe his music I'd love to be able to say that I saw it coming; that this whole episode was somehow presaged in his flood of terrible hit songs. But I'm unable to make this claim. I listened back to a few of his bigger hits today while writing this article, to be sure there was nothing there I had previously missed. Nope, not a thing: the same limp, anodyne trash as it always had been from the mouth of Noah. He must have been bottling all of that negativity up inside – too bad. If he had let some of it out, it would have been a kill two birds type of victory: no bombing, so all of those kids would still be alive, and we would have had a decent rocker in our lives these past few years instead of the Noah Hastings we all knew and detested.

I went the next day to visit my daughter in the hospital. Her smile when she awoke told me most of what I needed to know. I thought about telling her about what had happened at the Garden the previous evening, but she's too young (just) to have been interested in Noah Hastings and his awful music, and given that, there was no real reason to tell her about the pointless death of almost a hundred innocent kids while she was still recovering her fluid balance. After a little while, a doctor came in and told us we could go home. As we walked out of the A&E to head back downtown, I realized that some of the victims of the Hastings bombing had been routed to Mount Sinai for identification. I saw a man and woman, both looking to be in their late thirties, clinging to one another for dear life, sobs shaking each of them violently. I had brought my daughter to the hospital worried and had gotten lucky; some other parents obviously hadn't had the same fortune. I instantly felt guilty again for having missed the concert via divine intervention, as I grasped my daughter's tiny hand as tight as I could without alarming her.

'Right when we didn't need it, America's relationship with Islam gets more complicated', by Nina Hargreaves, *Washington Telegraph*, June 22nd, 2021

The FBI confirmed this morning what many had already hypothesized: that Noah Hastings was inspired by radical Islamism in perpetrating the bombing at Madison Square Garden on the 16th of this month. For those of us who feared the societal problems speculation on this subject was creating already, today's announcement is particularly worrying.

Although conjecture around a link between radical Islamism and the Noah Hastings bombing began almost immediately after the MSG incident for no other reason than an 'if the shoe fits' mentality in relation to these matters in American life, details about the contents of Hastings' dressing room from the night of the incident poured fuel on the fire. A copy of the Koran was found there, as well as other books dealing with the subject of radical Islam, including Abdul Salam Zaeef's *My Life with the Taliban*. Admittedly, there was an eclectic bunch of literature found in Hastings' temporary abode – *Mein Kampf* was also one of the books found amongst the detritus. Yet the existence of the Islamic theme of at least a small but notable group of books found in with Noah Hastings' belongings is difficult to ignore, even for those most willing to search hard for another culprit – *any* other culprit – out of political, social or religious considerations.

There is also the detail that, while not having been confirmed as such by today's announcement, nevertheless gains credibility by association, concerning Noah Hastings having met with a Los Angeles-based imam on the day of his suicide. The man in question, Amir Elahi, does indeed exist, runs a mosque in West Hollywood, and had flown into New York on June 16th – and out again that same afternoon. While a truly credible witness confirming Hastings and Elahi being together on June 16th has yet to emerge, there are hearsay reports placing the two in each other's company on that day.

Details are thin in the FBI press announcement. It simply tells us that the Bureau has amassed enough evidence to believe that radical Islam was the motivating factor in the bombing and that as a result, radical Islamist terrorist groups may well have been involved. Several have already jumped to take credit in the wake of the FBI's announcement, such as the Islamic Brothers for American Jihad. This will seemingly form the core of the investigation the FBI have launched into whom Noah Hastings' accomplices might have been, if any, in relation to the bombing which took place on Wednesday, June 16th.

As a result of the FBI's announcement, Sarah Simpson, the White House Communications Director, was forced to answer questions on the topic late this morning. She was understandably vague, only venturing to tell us that the president is fully supportive of the Bureau's investigation into the matter. A follow-up question around whether the White House was worried that there could be similar incidents in the near future, perhaps even copycat crimes, was then put to Ms Simpson. She closed the press conference without answering.

The FBI formalizing the premise that radical Islam was at the very least the inspiration for the Noah Hastings bombing – if not the direct cause via other sinister third agents – will take an already out-of-control situation and introduce full-blown meltdown. Yesterday evening, Dwayne Fairchild, the stunt double from the Hastings monkey movie made a few years ago, felt the need to go on national television to demonstrate the fact that he was still in one piece. While I'm sure Mr Fairchild's supposed rationale for appearing on

15

the evening news is at least partly undone by obvious self-interest – anyone with any connection to Noah Hastings is crawling out of the woodwork at the moment, unsurprisingly – it does indicate the degree to which the speculation has quickly gone from the sublime to the ridiculous. Sadly, the appearance of Mr Fairchild on a mainstream TV channel demonstrating for all to witness his ongoing biological capabilities was not enough to silence conspiracy theorists of the 'stunt double' strain; almost as soon as Dwayne had disappeared from our screens, social media outlets were filled with discussions that were highly irrational, even by the low standards of the previous week. My personal favourite example revolved around a blog piece that wished to advance the theory that the man who had claimed to be the stunt double was in actual fact Noah Hastings himself (!). I need to comment that while Dwayne does look a lot like Noah Hastings from behind (as you would expect for a stunt double), facially they don't even look particularly similar.

If that is where we were collectively as a nation before the FBI confirmed our worst fears – thinking that Noah Hastings is hiding right in front of our faces, alive and well – I can only begin to imagine what the tone of the conversation around the Hastings bombing will be now that the Islamic link has been all but confirmed by the announcement. In an age of raging sensitivities to issues around racial and religious identity, I fear that a pop star committing suicide in the name of Allah could act as a trigger, releasing untold pent-up pressure from within our collective social consciousness. In other words, once it becomes all right to take a swing at Islam again, even in liberal circles, what other current sacred cows could become roast beef? Sexism in the office place? Homophobia in previously liberal circles? The N-word becoming okay for white people to use anew?

To some of you, I might have sounded as paranoid in that last paragraph as many of the social media obsessives I casually denigrated earlier in this article. Or that I am showing my true colours as a member of the 'MSM'. Perhaps I am being paranoid – I sincerely hope that I am. Yet I cannot help but fear that the Madison Square Garden bombing, and the reopening up for consideration America's relationship with Islam that is bound to follow today's FBI announcement, will have a rhizomic effect on this country's political correctness debate; hatred branching out into previously off-limits regions faster than we can even digest, never mind try to control.

I will end on a disclosure I am uncomfortable making: I'm glad I'm not a Muslim at the moment. If I'm willing to say that in the *Washington Telegraph* today, I shudder to think what others might say online tomorrow.

Excerpt from the book, *Noah Hastings and the End of America*, by Slovakian intellectual Jadran Babic, published August 2021

First and foremost, like every historical event that lingers in the popular collective consciousness, we must first view the Noah Hastings concert incident (which popular culture will surely invent a short, catchy nickname for soon enough – 'Hastings Wednesday', an early and rather lame suggestion, has thankfully not found currency) through the lens of Marxism.

Once the causality of the event had been determined beyond doubt, Hastings and everything he had ever been involved in became immediately and irrevocably *verboten* in the United States. There was no other possible outcome. Here was a fresh-faced young man, the very personification of child-friendly, harmless, capitalist entertainment; and he, in the end, turned out to sympathize with what is seen through American eyes as the most evil, pernicious creed in the entire world, that of fundamentalist jihadism. Hastings had to be demonised, made into an aberration, some sort of tumour on the face of American popular culture that they had failed to recognize due to its cunning deviance. That an older demon in the American ideological framework, the spectre of Marx, has been completely overlooked is no surprise. But it lingers in the US subconscious, and long after the shock of the Muslim connection wears off, Americans will have to wrestle with the Marxist icon that was always lurking in their midst, taking on the clothes of the capitalist *struktur*. It is only then that the Americans will understand the events of June 16th in their full context.

If one looks at the promotional video for Hastings' song, 'I'm Going to Dance Until Late, Late, Late' (coincidentally, the last song Hastings ever sang, pushing the button on the explosive device he was attached to during its duration at what was to become his final concert), it is instructive as to how the Marxist framework within his oeuvre works. At the beginning of the video, Hastings is seen in stereotypical working man's clothes, the uniform of the proletariat. This is meant to signal, with subtlety I might add sarcastically here, that Hastings is a 'normal guy'. While this is important to the way the rest of the piece plays out, it is also meant to signify Hastings' lack of material wealth. He enters a proletarian bar and orders – what else? – a beer. A 'brewski' as one of this class might call it. At this point, a non-creatively imagined version of Satan appears in the bar. You can imagine what I am talking about even if you have never seen this video. This devil is wearing a red leather top, has a forked tail, horns on her head and is holding a pitchfork. Ah, I hear you say, at least the typical gender identification with the 'Prince of Darkness' has been inverted. But of course, when you make the devil a woman, certain rules must then be observed. She has to be dressed in a revealing manner, one that makes her as sexually appealing to men as possible. In essence, she must be a whore. The devil invites Noah Hastings into the gentlemen's toilets – known as 'the office of Satan' in common American parlance, incidentally – and there, behind a stall door, Noah and Beelzebub kiss romantically. This meeting of the mouths clearly seals some kind of a deal because as they part lips Hastings is magically transported to a mansion in Los Angeles, somewhere like Malibu perhaps, which is filled with a lot of wine bottles and women dressed in revealing bathing costumes. Opulence, in other words: this is what is clearly signified here. Hastings walks around by the outdoor pool of this mansion, not believing his luck, engaging in fairly crude yet able to get past American censors-level behaviour with several of the half-clothed females in attendance. He then walks into his new kitchen and discovers that he has several servants. He slaps one on the head and demands something – the servant then scurries away and comes back promptly with beer served in a diamond-studded glass. The message here is interesting: despite having come up in the world, the character Hastings is playing in the piece has not changed his tastes whatsoever. He wants the same beer he had in the proletarian bar, this time served in a glass that happens to be priceless. This is signifying that the proletariat, and in particular the *lumpenproletariat*, can never truly become bourgeois. It is for this reason that they, in essence, deserve their poverty. The argument is that they couldn't, or at least wouldn't, enjoy the fruits of a better lifestyle and simply pine for the simple things they already have access to, only framed within a more opulent *rahmen*. While I can certainly believe that Hastings himself had no knowledge of any of the obvious political ideas contained within the video, I refuse to countenance the notion that those who were directly involved in the design and production of this piece of advertising were unaware of the Marxist ramifications of the work that they were presenting.

The video's denouement has the Hastings character confronted by the leather-clad Baroness of the Underworld, who now wants his soul in return for the gorgeous girls in bathing suits-laden palace on the Californian coast. But the pop singer simply snaps his fingers, which in turn causes his servants to come running, dragging Satan away and throwing her into a dustbin outside. Oddly, I have perhaps never seen a better display of what Marx's idea of historical materialism means, leading me to believe that whomever scripted the video must have read (or at least skimmed) *Das Kapital*. Wealth is so powerful here it can be used against anything; even the force which allowed that wealth to accumulate in the first place. A woman who controls all evil in the universe is no match for the might that can be bought with a surplus of filthy lucre, in other words. Marxist ideas here, it almost goes without saying, are obviously inverted, distorted so that they fit in with a pro-capitalism message. What could be more American than the idea of defeating evil through money?

That this is one of the clearest displays of historical materialism in American popular culture over the last decade, albeit in a perverted form, I have no doubt. But there are other examples in both Hastings' audio and video work that demonstrate the same messages, turning Marxism on its axis. In fact, one could say that his entire oeuvre is little more than a propaganda tool for pumping out the American pro-capitalist agenda. People have said that Noah Hastings' music was not creative in the slightest; on this, I beg to differ. It is difficult to say the same thing in slightly different ways over one hundred times – however, the Hastings back catalogue achieves this feat with flying colours. In the lyrics to Hastings' 2015 hit, 'I Love the Way that Your Love Loves Love', Hastings spouts the following verse:

I love the way that love follows love
And I love the way that your love follows mine
If you were to give all of your love to me
I'd be yours until the end of time

Ignore the clunkiness of the phraseology, or the fact that 'mine' and 'time' do not rhyme. In crude, almost monosyllabic terms, this verse sets out the way love is commoditised under the capitalist system. Interpreting such a barbaric text may be trying, but useful nonetheless. The first line tells us that love begets more love – switch out 'love' for 'money' and you are there. Taking love to mean money throughout the rest of the piece, Hastings here is talking about how in a neo-liberal economy 'her love' can follow his. In other words, Hastings has been allowed by the loss of communitarian spirit that would have defined his masculinity in other societies to marry for money. But part and parcel of this arrangement is the fact that Hastings does not need to follow through. Just as the female Satan can be dumped into the dustbin (literally) when Hastings is through with her, despite having kept her side of the bargain, the idealised woman in 'I Love the Way that Your Love Loves Love' will ultimately be thrown out with the rubbish – metaphorically or literally, we have to wait and see. Within a commoditised culture, the method by which the disposal takes place is largely irrelevant in the end.

All of this makes the manner of Noah Hastings' demise intriguing indeed. It is as if in destroying himself in the name of something that America despises deeply he was attempting to atone for his past sins; for the endless videos he pumped out propping up the moribund western system and its values. It will be interesting to see how Hastings' work is now taken up as we move into a post-capitalist society. Indeed, the manner of his death now makes what was once a fairly routine and dull body of work into something worth analysing for further clues about the future of America.

June 16th, part one (The Man with the Dogs)

Noah wakes up that morning with what feels like a mild hangover. This is odd to him, given that he recalls having been raging drunk the previous evening and, truth be told, inebriated for most of the previous day. The drinking began on the way to NYC and then didn't stop once he'd landed. He tries to remember returning to his hotel room, whenever in fact he did so; he cannot recollect anything about it for the time being. Looking into the mirror at the massive bags under his eyes, Noah's mind suddenly brings forth something revelatory, nothing to do with the events of last night but significant to a weighty decision he had made: *today is the day I will die.* The thought makes him tingle all over in anticipation, causing his energy level to rise.

This revelation aside, he still finds the whole previous day prior to boarding the flight extremely blurry; difficult to remember even in the broadest detail. *There was no show. That's why I can't remember shit.* On the days when he had no crowd to perform for, Noah sailed through everything, trying to exist and nothing else for the whole of the twenty-four-hours in which there was no screaming fan base in front of him to boost his ego back into working order. As a result, the whole thing always felt a bit like the Greek version of the after-life: a hazy, grey affair that was shapeless and meaningless. It was thus easy to consign to oblivion.

A memory from last night suddenly jumps out at Noah from the semi-hungover blue: sitting through a boring dinner with a journalist he had never cared for from one of those hip rock mags that constantly criticized his music. Worse yet, along for the ride was a

23

groupie type he'd shaken off months previous, brought as a guest of the dull writer. Also in train was a man Noah had not been formally introduced to, but whom he had assumed was another unvetted accomplice of the rock journo, who'd brought into the restaurant with him a pack of dogs on leashes; terrifying-looking canines that kept trying to eat things off of all the adjacent tables. The Man with the Dogs, much to Noah's annoyance, kept attempting to be overly familiar with him throughout the tedious dinner, touching his arm extremely often and using the phrase, 'Noah, as old friends, you and I both know . . .' over and over again.

Noah thinks more about this memory and then comes to the conclusion that he must have dreamt it all. *I always feel better when I wake up in the morning having had fucked-up dreams regardless of what I've drunk or taken the night before, don't I?* Noah has noticed this tendency for the first time. He then reflects on how it was strange that no aspect of the monumental decision he'd made on the plane ride from LA to New York yesterday morning had made its way into his nocturnal imaginings. *Perhaps I just don't remember those dreams.*

It is at this point that Noah first realizes how sweaty he is. He is actually literally drenched in his own bodily fluids, his perspiration dripping onto the carpet like a faulty bathroom tap, as if he'd been for a heavy jog or played a particularly onerous game of tag football. He concludes quickly that the reason for this is the same as it was for so many things these days: his age. *Twenty-five. Metabolism changing. The heat my body generates while I slumber reminding me that I'm getting closer and closer to thirty.* Noah then breaks into a large smile at where his thoughts had led him. He would never be thirty. He would never even be twenty-six. How does the saying go? Live fast, die young and leave a good-looking corpse. This makes Noah laugh out loud; he would have to make an exception for the last of these specifications.

He towels off and then pulls on some clothes. Noah decides to head downstairs to have breakfast in the hotel, clammy skin be

24

damned. This is unusual behaviour for the pop star, being seen in public looking this dishevelled. Several of his LA neighbours had made headlines by going out their front doors looking like a bag of crap, and Noah had long vowed to be much more cautious himself. But since the decision on the plane had been taken – and the fact that he was in New York; no matter how long he had left to live, he would never have had the balls to walk into a public space in Los Angeles dressed like a homeless person – he has decided to loosen up a bit. If he is caught on camera there will be speculation amongst the journos this morning that he has been boozing again. *Good. They'll think they have something for tomorrow's papers until what happens tonight goes down.*

Noah steps into the elevator and thinks for a moment of his little entourage. *Jules will go apeshit when he finds out what I'm doing, going to breakfast all alone looking like I spent the night sleeping in the alleyway behind the hotel. Murray will have a dump in his underpants too.* He doesn't meet a soul on his way down to the lobby and only when he gets to the entrance of the hotel restaurant does he encounter some fellow breathing souls.

'Mr Hastings, so glad you can join us this morning. Please, have your pick of the tables.'

The host is obviously a heterosexual man in his early thirties and thus has no interest in Noah Hastings beyond his professional duties. He gives his offer of tables to the world-famous pop singer in a hospitality sector worker, I-could-give-two-fucks-who-you-are voice. Noah points to a table in the far corner while saying nothing. The host simply nods, subconsciously following the non-verbal bid for silence, and begins to walk in the appointed table's direction. Noah follows, meanwhile scouting the terrain: no press at the front of the hotel, or indeed inside of it. He supposes it's a little early yet. This isn't normal for him, getting up first thing, so he can understand the hacks not bothering to turn up until a little later. He also reminds himself that this is New York City he's in, not Kansas City or Dallas or Tallahassee, so by default the minutiae of his day becomes automatically less newsworthy to the pea-brains trying to make a living shoving a camera up his behind. At least this is what Noah is telling himself to keep the fear at bay, the terror that perhaps he has reached his 'Andrew Ridgeley moment', on absolutely the wrong day: ahead of the evening that would contain his biggest ever statement to the world.

Andrew Ridgeley was 'the other guy' in Wham! – the one who wasn't George Michael. A possibly apocryphal story goes: one night near the end of his fame's twilight, Ridgeley was exiting a London nightclub, one frequented by pop stars and so thus staked out by paparazzi. As he left for the evening, the musician prepared himself for what he thought was going to be the inevitable crush of photographers; a slight duck of the head and a raising of one side of his jacket to shield his face and that of his date. But on this occasion, the assembled hacks simply let Ridgeley walk by them, unimpeded by any invasive lenses in the face. They had all agreed to form a collective front with the view of informing Mr Ridgeley about his sell-by date having arrived. Poor Andrew got the message, loud and clear; he was famous no longer, the hacks had declared it. This event loomed large in the psyche of Noah Hastings (he saw it described on TV once, not long after his first brush with fame), essentially having become his pet phobia. He was terrified of it far more than death. Dying is simply the end of life. Being forced to live on knowing your fame has been stripped away is far, far worse in Noah's opinion.

'Good morning, what can I get you?' the woman who is to be Noah Hastings' waitress says mere seconds after he takes his seat. The hotel restaurant is rather bereft of customers at this early an hour. He takes in her visage; she looks to Noah to be in her late twenties. She clearly doesn't recognize the famous singer in the slightest. This causes his panic to resurface, mere moments after he had got it under control.

When he had first risen to public awareness, Noah found almost everyone knowing automatically who he was to be alarmingly perplexing. The idea that he hardly ever had to introduce himself anymore, to anyone, was difficult to adapt to for a long time, perhaps up to a year after he'd made it. But the phobia-related panic attacks had started a little after that first year of fame had run its course. *It's funny; I never had any time where I enjoyed the attention for what it was. I went from it freaking me out immediately to freaking out if it didn't happen on the rare occasions that I found myself not recognized.*

'Are you okay, sir?' the waitress asks him. *Jesus, do I look that bad this morning? And she still has no fucking idea who I am.* Noah gets a sudden impulse, one that he decides to roll with.

'*I'm fine, my little darling one,*' he sings, a line from one of his more well-known hits, in a slightly rough around the edges version of what he does on stage most nights. The waitress simply stands there in front of him, baffled as to why her clearly hungover customer is crooning all of a sudden.

'Yes, I'm fine, thanks,' Noah finally says simply to move the situation along as the waitress refuses to break the silence following his now clearly ill-advised warbling. 'Can I have the special, please?'

'Special one, two or three, sir?'

'I don't mind, just use your imagination.'

This sort of answer usually does the trick, as waiting staff aren't keen on upsetting a celebrity. But this woman has absolutely no idea the person she's serving happens to be a world-famous pop star and so she stands her ground, baffled by the last reply to which she was subjected.

'Sorry, sir, but they are all different. If you could let me know which one suits you, I'll be happy to get that to you as quick as can be.'

Christ, how embarrassing. This is the problem with fame – it's a bit like crystal meth. Wildly amusing at first but gets old fast. Only by that time you're heavily addicted and need ever increasing doses of it just to make you feel normal enough to continue with your day.

The other shitty thing about fame is that it's the nth degree of something. Once you achieve fame and still aren't happy with your life, where the hell is there to go next? Fame was supposed to have healed all of Noah's wounds, particularly the ones gained from having had the 'interesting' childhood that he'd had. It was supposed to have let him feel good about himself once again after his abusive dad had crushed his ego over the course of a couple of agonizing decades. You would have thought that selling out arenas the world over would have made Noah feel redeemed, the one who was in the right all along; but no, in some ways it had made him feel even more insecure than he had previously felt. He would often have little panic attacks when he was on stage. *You're a fraud, Hastings. You know you are. Someday, someone is going to walk up on stage, kill the sound, and tell you the joke's over. You can go back to being the laughing stock with the fucked-up daddy again.* Moments like these, facing the stunned, ignorant face of a hotel restaurant waitress, brought home how transient the whole thing was; not only fame but everything, including love and meaning.

Noah now desperately needs something to get himself out of the funk he's managed to slump into. Searching his mind for what might do the trick, he recalls the fact that he is going to kill himself on stage that very evening, murdering as many of his fans as he can along the way; this perfectly does the trick. Noah immediately cheers right up, as if the two little panic attacks he had subjected himself to had never even occurred at all. He then scans the waitress' nametag: Emma.

'I'll have the number three please, Emma,' Noah says with a sudden megawatt smile. Satisfied that an unpleasant transaction is finally at an end, but still slightly disturbed by the dishevelled yet still admittedly good-looking man from whom she'd taken an order, Emma bounces off back to the kitchen. This leaves room for another waitress, one theoretically serving another table in the restaurant, when and if another table full of hotel guests should ever come downstairs looking for a meal, to creep up to Noah's table looking like a Christian pilgrim who has laid eyes on the Shroud of Turin.

'Can I just say that I'm, oh God you have no idea . . .'

This waitress, needless to add, does indeed know who Noah Hastings happens to be. She has decided, almost certainly unconsciously, to park herself at what is an odd distance from the pop singer's table. Not far enough away to be in any way a socially comfortable distance, yet not close enough to be where you would normally take someone's order from, or even initiate a conversation, were you to try and do either of those things. She then starts to gently rock backwards and forwards on the balls of her feet. Tears slowly form in her eyes, in a manner eerily reminiscent of the way they do for a toddler when it doesn't get its way. This weeping waitress looks to Noah as if she might be on the verge of a seizure.

'I can see you're a fan,' Noah says, overjoyed in a way he would be embarrassed to admit to absolutely anyone he knew. He loves to get that hit of adulation in his hour of need, like a crack addict finding a dirt-covered piece of rock under a cushion. 'Would you like me to sign something?'

'Uh yes, my arms. My legs. My belly? My whole damn body! No, no, just kidding!'

Noah feels his stomach turn slightly, his buzz almost completely killed. He recognizes the waitress' southern accent and puts the whole package together. *White trash, trying to make it in New York. As an actress most likely, but settling for porn from day one.* After the awkwardness of the 'sign my body' routine, the misplaced southern belle of course can't think of what to follow up with to her idol, the man-god that is now looking at her like she'd thrown up all over him. Yet she can't bring herself to depart either, knowing she will hate herself for ever for having monumentally screwed up such a once-in-a-lifetime opportunity. Instead, she stands in stoic silence, staring at Noah fixedly. Noah looks at her more closely and has a sudden change of heart. *She's kind of hot. Maybe I should try and get in her pants after all*. This thought is then interrupted by his actual waitress, Emma, the one who had no idea who the hell he was, coming back with coffee in hand, clearly part of the special number three that Noah had blindly ordered.

'Darlene! Aren't there customers to attend to?'

'No, there ain't, ma'am.'

Darlene has a point.

'There you go, sir.'

Emma places the coffee down in front of Noah with this pleasantry. She then looks from Darlene to Noah and back to Darlene again, before turning once more to her customer and saying:

'Sorry, sir, is Darlene here causing you any dismay?'

Noah has to smile at the officiousness of Emma's language. *Clearly harbouring dreams of one day being the HR director in a large corporation. I like a girl with some ambition. Maybe I should try and get into Emma's pants instead.* These are all idle thoughts from Noah, mental farts almost. He knows even while he is thinking these things that there is no way on Earth he's going to try and sleep with either waitress. Imagine if one of them turned him down? Not worth considering the horror.

'Darlene is fine right where she is, thanks,' Noah says, wishing to prolong the entertainment. Emma looks at Darlene again and then back to Noah trying to figure out what the hell is going on. Deciding it's all beyond her, she turns around and goes back to the kitchen.

Five minutes later, when Emma returns holding a plate full of blueberry pancakes topped with bacon (*nice roll of the dice there, Hastings!*), Darlene is still standing in exactly the same spot, silently staring at Noah.

'Darlene, a tableful just walked in over there, into your section,' Emma says, grateful to have some control over the weird situation at long last. Darlene flashes sad eyes at Noah and then departs to do her job without another word. She begins a furtive wave and then stops, deciding it's probably inappropriate.

Darlene will be traumatized by this event for the rest of her life. She will look back with horror, thinking that perhaps if she could have found something to say to Noah Hastings on that fateful day, he wouldn't have done what he ended up doing. As if she was somehow partly culpable. It's a narcissistic train of thought, of course, and completely without an actual basis in reality, given Noah forgets all about her the second she is out of his eyeline.

Noah is about to start chowing down when his phone rings. He brings it out of his pocket to examine: Cheryl. *Shit. Better take it like a man. Be honest with her. Completely.*

'Hey, Cheryl.'

Sobs kick in immediately. Noah finds himself feeling slightly bad, despite himself. He suddenly wonders if he had drunkenly dialled her the previous evening without remembering; he puts such a possibility out of his mind due to the extreme horror of such a thing.

'That was colder than I was even expecting,' Noah's girlfriend says.

'Look, sorry, I have a lot on my mind at the moment.'

'What exactly do you have on your mind? Another woman?'

Cheryl's crudity of thought always disgusted Noah, but now more than ever. He decides to go for it.

'I'm going to kill myself on stage this evening.'

She laughs involuntarily. 'You're what?'

'I've got a bomb. I'm going to blow it up while I'm on stage tonight.'

She exhales. More of his stupid mind games, she thinks to herself.

'Look, I need some clarity on where we are, you and me. I can only avoid the press for so long.'

'I thought it was clear where we are.'

'Perhaps to you, not so much to me.'

'Like I said, I'm committing suicide in a few hours' time. So, I leave it to you: would you prefer we were still officially an item when that takes place, or would you like it if we'd already formally broken up?'

31

'Right, that's it, Noah. I'm breaking up with you. Do you hear?'

'Works for me.'

Cheryl hangs up.

When Noah finishes his pancakes, during the eating of which he is watched every single, solitary moment by Darlene, staring through the kitchen porthole at the hero she had painfully humiliated herself in front of, he gets up from his table to head back to his hotel room. At this precise moment, Jules comes running into the dining area, takes a moment to make sure it really is his employer looking like a charity case and then dashes up to him, breathing hard all the way as if he had been running around for several minutes at pace looking for the pop star, which, of course, he had.

'Jesus, boss, don't do that to me.'

'Does Murray know I'm down here on my own?' Noah asks.

'Of course not. The girl on the lobby desk I recruited as a spy told me. Why didn't you call first?'

'It was early; I wanted to let you sleep a little longer.'

'Very kind, boss. But it's my job to make sure you're never alone.'

Noah laughs. The obsession the record company, Murray, anyone who surrounds him in this little cottage industry has with Noah never being solitary while in public for any period of time whatsoever strikes him as perhaps the most ridiculous aspect of his existence.

'I was hungry and I wanted to eat by myself, okay?'

'That's cool, boss. Just let me know next time, please?'

'Will do, Jules. I'm heading up to my hotel room now where I'd like to be alone. You see: now you've been informed directly.'

Jules pulls his 'concerned' face. 'Are you okay, boss?'

'I'm fine, Jules.'

A few months back, Noah got a little too close to Jules. They would hang out after the shows, go to clubs together; the line between employee-employer relationship and a friendship based on equality began to become blurred. Jules started becoming remiss in some of his duties, sure that his newfound friendship with Noah

32

suddenly meant he was above doing the menial tasks that filled most of his working day. Noah realized this and pulled back sharply. Jules has been acting a little bit the wounded puppy ever since.

When Noah gets back to his hotel room, his phone rings straight off. Looking at the display, Noah exhales sharply. Jules.

'I just saw you, like, three seconds ago.'

'I know, boss. But I forgot to remind you that you have a radio interview in the afternoon at KACL at two thirty.'

'What else is happening today?'

'Other than the show itself, nothing. Chill out, enjoy the Big Apple. Are the bodyguards with you or do you want me to give them a call?'

Silly Jules – worried again that Noah is going to go rogue.

'Don't worry about it. I'm going to hang in the hotel for a little bit. I can call Phil when I feel like going out.'

'Okay, boss. Have fun with yourself.'

Having fun with himself is precisely what Noah has in mind. The chief reason Noah was so annoyed at Jules having called him as he got into his room was that it ruined slightly what was for Noah always a moment of intense relief: finding himself once again alone in whatever hotel room he happened to be staying in. Ever since he had first found fame, this feeling had been with him whenever he'd been out in public. It was a little like someone who hates the cold having to go out into the Siberian winter and then returning to a heated indoor space. Privacy is valued at a higher and higher rate the more famous a person is – a golden rule. Noah turns on the television and uses the remote to discover what porn the hotel has on offer. Despite almost everything about his life, personal or otherwise, becoming shared with the world, Noah's porn addiction is the one thing absolutely no one has ever found out about (or so he thinks, as it's never been written about). He finds great solace in pornographic material, and the release he receives from masturbating to it is always far greater than even his most pleasurable sexual experiences with real life women.

This is one of Noah's deepest secrets, something he would never, ever tell anyone about, even in his most drunken or stoned hour. Before he had made it he thought that this was because he'd never been with the right woman; that once fame garnered him greater choice, he'd be sure to find the exceptional coital nirvana that had always eluded him. But sex post-stardom had actually turned out to be worse, if anything. It came down to simple personal space issues; with someone else there, one has to consider their wants, their needs, their desires, not to mention their barriers, their no-go zones. When Noah is by himself he can simply drift away into his own fantasy world without anyone else having to be considered. No one's bad breath, or unfamiliar body odour, or any other factor enters the equation. He can simply create his own sexual space to get off in. Noah once read that Elvis liked whacking off better than sex too, and although this was gleaned from a non-credible source, he had decided to believe it was true.

Despite the internet giving the modern porn consumer an almost limitless choice of material from which to toss off to, Noah prefers hotel porn over any other type of smut. He has never been able to fathom exactly why, but it remains the type of obscene material that gets him going most effectively. He uses the TV remote to scroll around the 'Adult Menu' until he finds a title that leaps right out at him: *Office Sluts*. Having never worked a white-collar job in his life, Noah has massive fantasies built up around what it must be like, and in particular the women one might work with in such a setting. He loves the look of a woman in a business suit and also the idea of a powerful lady as a concept – in the abstract anyhow. He clicks the icon 'BUY' and within two minutes, Noah knows he has picked well. A leggy blonde, Noah's type, walks into an office from the 1970s (although Noah is none the wiser on that front, having no idea whatsoever what a modern office interior actually looks like). She predictably has a few too many front buttons undone.

'Sorry, Mr Smith, are these the files you wanted?'

As she bends down to give the male porn star playing her boss an eyeful, Noah grabs himself for the first time that day. This will be a short viewing. He smiles as a thought occurs to him, seconds before release. *Is this the last time I'm ever going to jack off?* He tells himself, no, he'll manage to squeeze in one last go before show time.

Having spent himself during a scene in which the secretary is bent over the desk in what could only be described as a quasi-rape scene (she starts out asking her boss to stop but in true porn style, soon seems to enjoy it to the point of seemingly continuous orgasm), Noah immediately showers. This is something he always does following a session with himself; one of the few leftovers his brief dabbling with Islam has left him with is a fear of uncleanliness. As he stands under the hot water, which makes him feel much better about the world than he would have ever thought possible, Noah reflects back on his 'Muslim period', again a common ritual for him when he showers (the link between his need to be clean and his Islamic experiment being mostly unconscious on Noah's part but very much psychologically present).

He'd been heavily into drugs at the time, and pretty lame, quintessentially LA drugs at that: Seconal mostly, but also Nembutal. Downers, always downers, meant to keep the extreme anxiety he could never fully explain to himself throughout most of the adult portion of his life at bay. This was at the same time, oddly, as one of the few sections of his existence in which he had managed to be almost completely alcohol-free. Partly this was out of feeling that so long as he wasn't drinking he was doing no wrong; partly from a completely logical fear of accidentally killing himself via the infamously bad rock and roll combo of booze and barbiturates that had brought so many musicians to an untimely end.

Noah's constant need for chemical simulation at the time was also fired by the extreme boredom he was experiencing, always looking for something to stimulate him but coming up blank by looking in the usual places. He was between albums and tours, and some in the

35

media were even going so far as to question whether or not his career had permanently plateaued. One afternoon during this era, when he would have been so much better off using as the rare opportunity to get the hell out of town and sit on a beach somewhere in the Indian Ocean for a while, Noah found himself at a loose end as usual and decided to do what only the insane and/or terminally blasé would ever do while in the City of Angels: he decided to go for a walk. As he strolled down the sidewalks of Los Angeles, he found his thoughts turning to the extremely lame monkey movie he'd been roped into starring in, a film whose plot revolved around his pet escaping from the mansion and attempting to walk across LA. At a point during which his thoughts came back into the here and now after a long reverie which involved Noah trying to remember the name of the DoP who had worked on the monkey movie and failing to do so, a man he had come to hate on an almost pathological level during the making of said motion picture, Noah found himself directly in front of the entrance to a mosque. His first instinct was to laugh, simply at the fact that he no idea that a temple to Allah was so incredibly close to where he lived and yet he'd never bothered to notice it before. He walked in, mostly inspired by a pressing desire to remove himself from the repressive heat of southern California in mid-July. He must have cut an amusing figure to the few odd souls who were in that mosque off of Sunset Boulevard that summer's day – a strangely attired white male who looked as if he'd crossed the desert to get to their place of worship. He was mostly ignored by the denizens of the place, but as so often happened to Noah Hastings, destiny intervened. The imam, who in the normal run of things would not have been in the mosque on that particular day, caught sight of the beleaguered, wilted pop star. This imam would later say that the voice of Allah had instructed him to come to his place of work when he did, but this was extreme revisionism on the holy man's part; he'd actually come down because of a minor clerical issue that required his attention. He approached

Noah and greeted him in Arabic, on a whim. Noah looked at the imam, staring at him as if he were an apparition in a dream he couldn't make out what to do with. Finally, the imam said, in English:

'I get the sense you are looking for someone.'

That was all it took for Noah. He and the imam kicked off a sort of Yoda-Luke Skywalker flavoured friendship that would last two weeks shy of three months; seventy-five days when Noah was at the mosque for some portion of almost every single day. He immediately, that same afternoon he stumbled upon the mosque, stopped taking the downers and started to eat better. He approached his Koranic studies with a single-mindedness previously completely absent from his lifestyle. What drove him more than anything else was his long-standing, continuous search for a father figure, one to replace the shit dad he'd been lumped with by birth. In the history of this hunt, it always went thus: no one ever matched up in the end, and so the latest faux pere would be dumped and the search would continue anew. And so it transpired with the Sunset Strip imam. For a few months it looked as if it might actually last this time around.

From his end, the Islamic preacher was overjoyed to have such an unusual and committed disciple. He would always drop whatever he was doing to spend time with Noah, no matter what he'd been up to prior to the pop star's arrival at the mosque. This preferential treatment was not on account of Noah's fame, at least not at first; the imam actually had no idea that Noah was a celebrity as his student hadn't informed him of this fact and the imam sheltered himself from American popular culture as much as it was humanly possible to do so whilst living within the borders of Los Angeles County. That would all come later, near the end of their time together.

Noah kept his flirtation with Islam a secret from everyone, even Murray, his manager. He usually told Murray absolutely everything, mostly out of fear. *He always figures everything out eventually anyhow, so it's pointless to keep anything from him.* But this one thing Noah had stashed deep down (that and the penchant for hotel porn, obviously).

What was alluring about Islam, although Noah had never come close to admitting it to himself, was that it was forbidden, off-limits, decidedly un-American in the twenty-first century. At least according to people like his parents, which was what really mattered to Noah, who had been raised by two fundamentalist Christians. Their faith was based on a sort of Baptist meets Unitarian-style thing that had a tendency to wander wherever Noah's mother's medication took her, combined with wherever Noah's father's latest scam took the family geographically. For a while they were getting mail about how Jesus was still alive and living in Hawaii, or on the Moon in a futuristic development the Nazarene had called forth via a miracle. But as always, the disavowal soon followed. Literature excised, posters burnt, all mention of any belief stemming from the now-dead recent past forbidden in a way that would have impressed Orwell, always accompanied by yet another physical relocation. What always stayed, of course, was Jesus. Lovely, lovely Jesu. Everything else arranged itself around him, like the way all matter in the universe revolved around the Earth in the Hastings family's rather unorthodox viewpoint on astronomy. Jesus was both endlessly loving and brutally hateful, in that way that only makes sense to fundamentalist Christians. It was an upbringing that had left Noah with a burning, almost pathological hatred of Christianity and all of its accoutrements. His favourite number was six hundred and sixty-six.

Jim Crank, from a transcript of an excerpt from the July 3rd, 2021 episode of his daily, hour-long talk show, *God and Guns*

I always knew that kid was trouble.

Now I'm not going to sit here, patting myself on the back, saying, you know, 'I always knew Noah Hastings was an Islamic terrorist' or anything that dumb. But the fact that this has turned out to be the case can hardly come as a surprise to the millions of men and women across this great, God-blessed country we inhabit. That a traitor has been walking not only in our midst as one of us but has been filling our children's minds with anti-capitalist, anti-Christian messages for years and years now.

I know you're thinking, 'Come on, Jim. Sure, the kid turned out to be an evil SOB, but there was no way to tell that from his music, which was after all, you know, uh, innocence and flowers and what not.' Well, friends, I'll get to all that in a second here.

What I need to say first is that there are two demons stalking American life that I'm used to hearing, even from God-fearing, head-screwed-on-right conservative people I mean, are ones that I'm overplaying as threats. That yes, they aren't ideal, but come off it, Jim, they aren't the goshdarn horsemen of the apocalypse, are they now. I hope some of those people I've talked to over the past few years about these twin horrors that are trying to rip this great nation apart in front or our eyes can now realize that I was right all along. The duo of destruction I am referring to, of course, is popular music and Islam. And Lordy, they've finally come together in a terrifying way, have they or have they not?

Way back in the 1990s, I used to tell the great many listeners who would tune into my radio show week after week that popular music was the work of the devil, one that more than anything else was polluting the minds of our young children. This was when many people echoed my sentiments, even across mainstream liberal outlets. We saw the rise of the PMRC, a group founded to pressure the music industry into putting a rating system on albums in order to protect our most precious resource, our children. This was an organization this country has been the poorer for since its dissolution in my opinion, despite it being run by the wives of Democrat senators. You see, I can be non-partisan, you liberal hatemongers out there. Back then, we saw parents take to the streets and say that they would not accept any more filth being sold to their young ones. Back then, people took the threat that popular music posed to our fundamental Christian values seriously.

But then something happened in the middle of the 1990s. People started to lose sight of how pernicious the influence of popular music could be on the minds of our most precious resource. I started to hear, 'Oh Jim, you worry too much' a whole bunch. This all got worse after the events of September 11th, 2001, when, to some extent understandably, people in America forgot all about the terrors of pop music because the spectre of a world run by Islamic fundamentalists suddenly came into clear view. I could live with this because I had been telling people for many years by that point how dangerous Islam was; what a threat it posed to America and its values. I'd had to suffer for years in the lead-up to the events of September 11th, 2001, you know. People calling into my show, my listeners, hardworking, conservative people remember, and they would say, 'Jim, why do you worry so much about the Muslims? They live in all these disorganized places, with no civilization. What threat do they pose to us?' And these people got their answer. Two towers of fire as a gone-dunnit answer, my friends! Oh Lord, why didn't the people listen to me beforehand and recognize the great Satan that was clearly in their midst? Why did it take people having to watch half of lower Manhattan go up in flames to recognize that Islam was such a danger to us and our values?

But then, with time, even people's worries about Islam faded away. After all, there were no more attacks on home soil – thank you again for that, George W – so people thought the great Satan had been conquered or shown to be a paper tiger who had managed to get lucky one horrible, never to be forgotten September morning. And once again I told the people all about it, again and again, not fruit smoothie-gulping liberals I'm talking about here, but the fine old folks who tune in to my show week in, week out, working their fingers to the bone the rest of the time, Republican as can be, an elephant tattooed onto their hearts. My people, you see, and I told them how the threat of Islam was still out there, waiting, crouching like a bearcat in the jungle. And these people, these God-loving, Jesus-worshipping, taxpaying people, they would say to me, 'Oh Jim, you worry too much. George W went over there and whupped them all up.' That's what they said to me, those I'd-kiss-George-Washington's-gosh-darn-corpse-if-I-could-lay-my-cotton-picking-hands-on-it people who call into my show. That Islam was no longer a 'going concern'. Well, we saw where such a lax attitude, even amongst livin' in wait for the day of redemption, flag-lovin' Americans, got us. Our children dying in the smoke of a bomb attached to an Islam-infested coot, excuse my language there, singing his devil-minded songs before taking them out, blood a-spewin' every which way.

We watched a few weeks back the two great devils in modern society come together to take the lives of ninety-one of our most precious resource. I knew the day would come. And I don't want to say I told you so. But, my friends, I told you so.

A *Scope* magazine debate: 'Have we decided
incorrectly on the motivation behind the Hastings'
Madison Square Garden bombing?',
August 2021 edition

As regular readers will know, every month *Scope* magazine picks a
topic du mois and pits two opposing points of view against each other
to debate the issue. This month, we are pleased to have with us
Mohammed Qasim, noted author, journalist, and director of the
think tank, Policy Institute for Liberal Thought. He will be up
against *Washington Telegraph* commentator Nina Hargreaves. These
two prominent guest writers will be discussing whether or not we
have jumped to the conclusion that Islam was the primary motivation for the Hastings bombing too quickly, and if and how we should
remain open minded about what influenced Noah Hastings to commit murder/suicide on June 16th, 2021.

Dear Nina,

*As you know, I was born in Boston, Massachusetts to a couple who had left
Pakistan only a few years before my birth. My parents departed from Asia
with the hope of a better life, not just for themselves but obviously for their
children as well. As it happens, my father succeeded beyond his wildest
dreams. His tailor's shop became the place to go for an expensive-looking
suit that you didn't have to pay Newbury Street prices for. Eventually, he
was able to open a small chain of shops in the tri-state area.*

*Thinking back on my childhood, I can't recall a single time when I
was singled out for the colour of my skin or my religion. It helped,*

obviously, that I was in both a socio-economically high market and internationalist surrounding to some extent, but having said that I also do not recall having encountered any Islamophobia in the American media whatsoever during this time. I wasn't even aware of the term, actually. The fact that there was a distinct word for hatred of the religion I had grown up with, I did not discover until I was seventeen.

This is because I turned seventeen in 2001. And then everything changed. You cannot begin to imagine the impact the events of September 11th had on Muslim-Americans unless you experienced it first-hand. Even among my friends I was being asked why we, the moderate Muslims, would not 'stand up and be counted'. Suddenly, I was being implored to denounce my religion on a continuous basis by even my dearest friends.

Despite not being particularly religious, I feel culturally Muslim, deeply in fact, and felt no reason in late 2001 as to why I should have to give all that up simply because a gaggle of Saudi maniacs who happened to nominally share the same faith as me had flown some planes into a couple of buildings in Lower Manhattan.

Now, once again, something terrible, something inexplicable has come out of nowhere – and it is all Islam's fault. Again. When I first heard the FBI announcement, I reasoned that it wouldn't, it couldn't be as bad as post-9/11 had been. And yet it so far feels even worse. It is as if people feel like they let their guard down, allowed themselves to think that nothing like 9/11 could ever possibly happen again and then suddenly, out of nowhere, they have been shown how wrong they were in thinking so.

All of this on the basis of a vague press announcement from the usually not particularly trusted FBI. Could we at least wait to hear some solid evidence before we demonize a large minority of Americans all over again?

Mohammed Qasim

Dear Mo,

As a cherished friend of mine for over ten years, I know first-hand of the emotional turmoil you have suffered via an Islamophobia that has never truly departed from this country following the events on September 11th, 2001. I have witnessed the outrageous slurs that are the backdrop to your professional life. Yet what we are not here to discuss today is whether or not American Muslims being subjected to religious persecution is a bad thing. That, we should all be able to agree, is an extremely regrettable element of twenty-first-century American life. What we are here to talk about is whether or not we are being hasty in declaring that Noah Hastings was inspired – even in a warped fashion – by the tenets of Islamist fundamentalism in doing what he did as a final act. This query, my friend, you have not even tried in the slightest to deal with in your opening statement. As a result, you have left it for me to say what needs to be said. Unfortunately, it appears to be all but certain that Noah Hastings had been affected by exposure to jihadist influences, and that his interest in Islamism played some part in why he decided to carry out the acts of June 16th.

Evidence placing Amir Elahi and Noah Hastings together in New York on the day of the bombing is now overwhelming, as is proof that Hastings had attended Elahi's mosque many times before, something he had kept secret even to those who knew him best. The literature found in the dressing room could be random, but the links with the LA imam are certainly not. I wish this were not the case as much as you do, Mo, but one cannot turn a blind eye to what the facts are telling us.

I do agree with you that the real issue here is why America has allowed the fact that Noah Hastings happened to be influenced by Islam in carrying out his horrific crime to become the catalyst for a renewed wave of Islamophobia that has poisoned public discourse. This is the real topic we should be discussing, you and I, right now. I'm afraid the idea that the Hastings bombing and Islam are not in any way related to one another is already a deceased one – whether you and I like it or not.

Nina Hargreaves

Dear Nina,

This past week, complete strangers have spat me at twice in the street and I've had excrement put through my home mailbox. Meanwhile, I have been subjected to so much hate mail at work from members of the public that the think tank I work for has had to take my details off of their website for the time being. This is a terrible professional kick in the teeth, and makes one understand what it must have felt like being a Jew in 1930s Germany: having your rights and your dignity taken away, bit by bit, one piece at a time.

Having said that, you are correct that I did not deal with the detail of the question put to us both sufficiently in my opening remarks, something I will correct with my follow-up.

All Islamic terrorist activities, indeed, all terrorist activities that are specifically ideologically motivated, need to be signposted. In other words, you need to do the deed and then make sure that everyone knows why it was done and to what end. Otherwise, what is the point? Why blow yourself up in the name of Islam or anything else if you're not entirely sure that everyone is going to understand the import of what you have done? This is totally absent in the case of the Hastings atrocity. The dubious Islamic Brotherhood for American Jihad group claimed responsibility for the attack shortly after the FBI announcement – but their involvement has already been publicly debunked by the Bureau. Apparently asked for eight basic facts about the bombing, they couldn't get even one of them correct.

Also, the clues that Noah Hastings left behind do not constitute proof in any legal sense. A copy of the Koran was found in the back-stage room he had occupied pre-concert, yes. Along with a Bible, a copy of Mein Kampf, and Steal This Book. Why is no one claiming in earnest that Noah Hastings was a yippie terrorist who did it in the name of Abbie Hoffman?

Hastings spent three months visiting a mosque in Los Angeles where he developed a friendship with the imam there. Three years ago. Visiting a mosque is not a crime in this country. At least, not last time I checked. It should also be stated for the record that having been questioned by the FBI, Amir Elahi himself remains a free man.

This appears to be all of the proof available surrounding the Hastings crime being linked to Islam. Obviously, we cannot know what information we are not at this time privy to that the FBI might have stashed away as its investigation continues. But I ask you this: surely if they are going to demonize a whole section of the American public (three million of us at last count), and not for the first time in this still young century either, at least give us more of an idea as to why they have reached the conclusion that they have done and felt confident enough to broadcast to the world.

Mohammed Qasim

Dear Mo,

Again, you open with a jeremiad on the evils of Islamophobia in America today. Again, I agree with you fully. This is not what we have come here today to debate. True, you have done better in attempting to state your case that we should remain open-minded about whether or not Islamism was a distinct influence in the Noah Hastings bombing on your second attempt. But I remain unconvinced, unfortunately.

Whether Hastings visited that mosque in LA three years before the bombing or three days prior, the fact remains that he did so. More damning is the fact that the imam of said mosque flew into New York the day of the incident, met with Noah Hastings, and then left town again shortly before the concert. The fact that the FBI do not have enough evidence to press charges against Mr Elahi does not mean he is innocent, nor that he does not have links to others who may been involved in the bombing. There are any number of reasons why the Bureau may have chosen not to hold the imam that do not involve him being completely uninvolved. You are also trapped in circular logic here:

46

if you are using the fact that the FBI *have not arrested Mr Elahi as proof that the Islamism charge is a false one, you are admitting that the* FBI *is acting as a rational agent. Yet they are still holding to the line that the crime was Islamically inspired, so you are back to square one.*

I wish I was wrong on this one, I sincerely do. But the evidence suggests strongly that Noah Hastings was inspired – if not aided directly by – the forces of jihadist Islamism when he took his own life and the lives of ninety-one of his fans.

Nina Hargreaves

Dear Nina,

It is not terribly surprising to me, sadly, that Islam is once again the whipping boy for all of the bad feeling that needs somewhere to go in the shadow of another American tragedy. What has given me cause for alarm is the precise way in which the wheel has stopped in front of the proverbial mosque again after the FBI *announcement. I have come to believe that many portions of the American establishment have a vested interest in seeing Islam as the bad guy, always and for ever. I never used to be paranoid on this subject. However, recent events have caused me to think again.*

I know this will strike many of you as coming from the conspiracy theory, lunatic end of American thinking before I even begin to say what I will say next. But say it I will: so long as it is simply Arabs killing other Arabs – Muslims killing other Muslims – in the Middle East, then every politician in Washington, Democrat and Republican, knows that to the vast majority of Americans it is and will remain a non-issue. It is only if and when Israel is under threat that it would suddenly become an urgent matter. The Pentagon knows that Israel's position at present is a lot more precarious than is believed, at least among the American general public who see it as essentially under no real immediate threat due to the way the emerging Shia-Sunni war in the Middle East has been reported thus far. The safety of Israel is never questioned in the American media; they tend to focus on whether our continued alliance with the Saudis is wise, or whether we would be better off pulling out of the region altogether. Both the Pentagon and the White House realize this is a long way from the reality, with both Sunni and Shia grasping that while each side intends to be the victors in this current, all-out jihad for ideological supremacy, taking care that Israel gets wiped off the map along the way is in both of their interests. Perhaps as a result of these factors, the military-industrial establishment has decided to whip up another round of Islam-hatred amongst the American public – and Noah Hastings and his bomb came along at just the right time.

I leave it to you to decide whether I'm being rational in starting to buy into this line of thinking or not. I'm willing to believe that perhaps I've lost perspective. Dog excrement through your mailbox can do that to a guy.

Mohammed Qasim

Dear Mohammed,

I could denounce you for plunging into borderline anti-Semitism with some of the implications of your theory. Instead, I will simply reiterate that all of the information we have accumulated so far points definitively to Noah Hastings having been directly influenced by Islamic jihadism, and furthermore that there is no solid proof which points us in a different direction. It is extremely regrettable that this is the case, and that this being so will almost certainly mean that a terrible case of Islamophobia settles across America for who knows how long a time. Yet I have always stuck to the facts, however unpleasant they may be, and I cannot make an exception in this case, however tempting that may be.

I would like you and I to work together with others to try and combat the vilification of Muslims that is already starting to occur as a result of the Hastings bombing. The evil stupidity of one deranged *ex-pop star should not unduly affect the lives of millions of Americans. Whatever the influence of Islam on Noah Hastings, we cannot allow such a thing to cloud our judgement of our fellow countrymen. I will do whatever is in my power to combat Islamophobia in the United States of America.*

Nina Hargreaves

'Could we please drop the whole "Islam is a religion of peace" garbage now?', by Patricia McShay, an article from the website *Bratbrey*, published August 11th, 2021

In the wake of the Federal Bureau of Investigation's revelation that the Noah Hastings bombing was in fact an act of Islamic aggression, and the subsequent, completely rational blowback the Islamic community in America has had to face, liberals in this country are up to their old tricks.

'It's not a war against Islam we should be talking about here,' says veteran communist hippie TV personality blowhard Mike Chuckshaw. 'There's a war going on within Islam itself. We need to help the moderates beat the extremists.'

This is classic liberal garbage. Any sane person knows there is no 'war inside Islam'. There are extremists, in other words people who are willing to either blow themselves up in the name of Islam like Noah Hastings, or to incite and indeed aid and abet others to do so. Then there are those I like to call the 'sub-extremists': Muslims who wouldn't go as far as the actual extremists, yet tacitly support their fellow Muslims in their jihad against western values and institutions.

Don't believe me that Islam as a religion is hell bent on destroying everything you and I hold dear? Let's examine the Muslims' sacred text for clues. The Koran mentions the need for jihad and the actions taken by Noah Hastings on June 16th explicitly. Talking about infidels, the Koran instructs Muslims that 'cursed they will be. Wherever they are found, they are seized and all slain' (33:61). An even better passage in the Koran on this topic is: 'slay the idolaters wherever you find them, arrest them, besiege them, and lie in ambush everywhere for them' (9:5). I could quote the Koran all day with stuff that backs up my point, but you get the message. Islam is not a religion of peace. I'll say it again: Islam is not a religion of peace. It is, and has since its inception been, a creed specifically aimed at the destruction of European and Judeo-Christian values.

In spite of the obviousness of everything I have just laid out, available to anyone with access to the internet, the liberal media has been inundating us with Islamic apologists since June 16th, all of them desperate to clear the good name of their little pet project. 'Why is America in such a rush to hate Islam?' asks long-time moron of the Left, Thomas Flannery. Uh, Jeez, Tom, maybe because they keep blowing up our children? 'Is the US Islamophobic?' asks perennial liberal cover merchants CNN. Let's see, libtards: not nearly enough, judging by the 'everyone hug a Muslim' spiel you pollute the airwaves with each and every day. I suppose these liberals are hoping that most Americans, particularly those who share their leftist creed, are ignorant of Islam's millennium-plus crusade against western culture; a never-ending, continuous 'holy war', if I may coin a phrase, involving direct military confrontations, genocide, sex with children, and pillage of both the literal and metaphoric kind. Then the liberals have the cheek to ask, in the shadow of almost a hundred dead American children in New York City, why we seek to demonize the sect who perpetrated the horror?

There's a war going on here, people, and wouldn't it be nice if the liberals shut up for once about how Islam is wonderful and cuddly and decided instead to back the side who are trying to defend the western values they supposedly share? I know, I know, I'm asking for far too much from the liberals. I guess when Islam takes over America and they're the first to be shoved off to concentration camps, places where they'll receive their 'Islamic re-education' programmes, they'll then realize the conservatives of this country might have been on to something this whole time.

An article from the website *Our Socialist Future*, by Kelly Ann McGregor, published August 18th, 2021

The investigation by the Federal Bureau of Investigation into the Noah Hastings bombing is the most perfect example of the capitalist corporate machine at work I have ever been witness to in all my short years. They go and announce to the world that the bombing was unquestionably the work of fundamentalist Islam. Then they arrest absolutely no one and manage to come up with no other credible lead in the weeks that follow. One could be tempted to say they simply jumped the gun; got worried about the vacuum of information out there and decided to fill it with something, anything. If so, why not go with the easiest thing for people to accept and say it was the Muslims again?

Except that this all runs too deep and is too powerful to simply be uselessness on the part of the FBI. The pinning of this tragedy on the already overburdened shoulder of America's persecuted Muslims smells to me of a deliberate attempt to smear Islam once again.

Perhaps the military-industrial complex wants to involve the US in the emerging war in the Middle East more directly. Maybe the Zionist Israeli government is crying out for us to help them go on building settlements on other people's land. Who knows, it could be anything involving the Jews.

The idea that Noah Hastings, the essence of a corporate, soulless, sell-out pop phenomenon, was a Muslim is absurd. Islam is a deep, spiritual religion, full of passion and wonder. It is the most beautiful religion one can imagine. That Hastings could have secretly been a Muslim while singing about his dick in not so subtle ways for years is not fathomable.

If they wanted to make it believable, they could have told us he had become a Zionist. I could have easily believed a Zio capable of blowing himself up and taking a hundred kids with him, no problem.

It's bad enough the corporate shills who run this country support the Zionists directly with their support of Israeli settlements; but trying to set Islam up for another fall is a step too far.

As a result of all of this going on in our society, I've organized a rally in LA for next Saturday, to start at 10 a.m. outside of Soho House on Sunset, proceeding up Sunset until we plan to get to the In and Out Burger for lunch around 1 p.m. If you're in the Los Angeles County area, please come and join us on Sunset at any point (we'll be the ones holding the signs that will say 'Islam = Feminism = Peace = Love'). Even Zios are welcome, so long as you are willing to repent your evil ways!

An article entitled 'Noah Hastings and the Zionist Military/Industrial Complex', from the August 2021 edition of *Beware the Lizards*, a publication run out of Austin, Texas, by the editor of the magazine (and sole contributor), Hitler Christ,

The Noah Hastings bombing and the events of September 11th, 2001 are strikingly similar in most respects. Both were mass terror events meant to shock and appal the greater American public; both were perpetrated by the government of the United States of America; both were blamed by the Washington administration on a bogeyman, which in both cases was Islam.

Why is the federal government so keen to have people in America hate Islam? Because they understand correctly, from CIA testing on the subject, that there is something deep within the western heart that fears Muslims. We see it in the crusades; we see it in C.S. Lewis' Calormen; always the Muslim is painted as something far beyond our comprehension. Meanwhile, truly exotic cultures like the Chinese are seen as placid, when in actual fact they represent much greater threats to our well-being and security.

As a result, they programme us from birth to hate Islam and then when they need to whip us into a frenzy of hatred, they push the right button. Works every time. They wanted to go to war in the Middle East in 2001 and so they blew up the towers in New York and blamed it on 'Islamic terrorists'. Then, twenty years later, they try and feed us a line about a pop star blowing himself up in front of a captive audience of his little teeny drones. The pop star explosion in the name of Allah is actually even more implausible than the

Twin Towers as not an inside job story, when you stop and think about it for two seconds.

It is interesting as well that all of this Noah Hastings stuff goes down when:

1. There's a major shitstorm brewing in the Middle East already in terms of internecine warfare.
2. Capitol Hill is besieged by Jews.

It was in fact a Jew, Hoffstein, the fall guy in the White House communications team who covered for the Federal Bureau of Investigation (another Zionist front) when they proclaimed Islam was once again trying to destroy America. This was not a coincidence. It was a clue given to us by the Zionist conspiracy of what their intentions are. They are toying with us all.

The aim of the game in 2001 was to draw us into an imperialistic war for oil in the Middle East, with the idea being to capture Iraq for America before moving onto Iran. Today, the aim is to convince the American public that we must get further involved in the current conflict in the Middle East because Israel is looking to be under increased threat. We've all been taught that Israel must be defended at all costs from a young age too, so you might think this would be unnecessary. But you'd be wrong because the American government never wants to be uncertain. The Jews that run this once great nation, now fallen into decadence, needed to be sure that the American people wouldn't cause any problems; that the road to a war in Palestine, stained with the blood of American troops, could go forward without a hitch.

People have asked who exactly that guy on stage on June 16th was, but I find the question to be tedious. Who cares? Some guy the American government paid to kill himself, with the promise of wealth for the family he would be leaving behind, probably some trailer trash on probation at the time. The Pentagon and the military-industrial complex can get anything they like, given their unlimited resources, all paid for by you and me, let us never forget that.

As for myself, and hopefully for all of you reading this, the war against the Zionist American deep state military/industrial complex soldiers onward. We need to look at events such as the FBI press release as positives: their mask is slipping off and soon all of America will be able to witness the lizard that lives underneath.

'No real news from the FBI – despite the hype' – Nina Hargreaves, *Washington Telegraph*, September 4th, 2021

There was a lot of build-up to today's FBI press conference, with rumours afoot that the Bureau might even be gearing up to announce that they had solved the Hastings bombing case in full, with culprits set to be named. Sadly, the payoff was a massive disappointment as a result. Despite a flurry of searching questions from the press corps, the FBI managed to come away having given away no new information of any real substance.

The fact that this press conference has been delayed twice over the last couple of weeks should have, in retrospect, rung alarm bells. It is clear that the FBI feels under intense pressure to make it seem as if they are making headway in a case that has captured the nation's imagination – the world's imagination, for that matter – without having anything real to show for a summer's worth of digging.

We were told that several suspects had been identified by the Bureau and that it was taking steps to both build a case and to protect the public from any further incident – although it is still too early to name anyone as the case against any one suspect or organization is at this point apparently 'nascent'. The FBI does remain sure that what they are chasing is a radical Islamist conspiracy to have committed the events of June 16th. They stressed that there are *certain* that this line of inquiry is correct, although the reasons for this are starting to feel thin. The Bureau needs to come up with some solid links that the Hastings bombing has to international Islamist terrorism quickly or else it will start to smell like a diversion at best, a perversion of natural justice at worst. Given the bombing almost certainly is connected in some way to Islamism, given the circumstantial details of which we are all aware of already, this step is all the more vital.

When asked about whether or not the imam who Noah Hastings had studied with – and with whom Hastings had met with on the day of the bombing – had been questioned again after having been taken into custody and released during the summer, the FBI were typically cagey. All they would say was that yes, Amir Elahi has been questioned again but no, he is not in custody for the time being. The reasons for this were not elaborated on. Yet the Bureau refuses to rule out Elahi as a primary suspect or at least an accomplice.

However, Elahi remains the only suspect that is known to the wider public. If a large-scale conspiracy was at work in creating the Hastings bombing, the Bureau had better start giving us some further names, and fast. The killer needs to be identified and brought to justice within a timeframe of weeks so that America can start healing the deep wounds caused by the Hastings incident. The longer the case persists in remaining unsolved, the longer this era of racial and religious tension in America will continue. Today's press conference offers no solace on this front. We could be in for the worst possible summer hangover.

- This *Washington Telegraph* story was originally printed and placed online with the final sentence reading 'We could be in for the worst possible Indian summer'. The *Telegraph* apologizes for any offence caused by use of this saying, which has now been removed, the article amended accordingly.

June 16th, part two (On your way to a Bilderberg meeting)

Noah climbs out of the hotel shower and walks out of the bathroom without towelling off, naked and dripping water all over the carpet. He is amused to see that *Office Sluts* is still playing; he had forgotten to shut it off. He has a momentary thought about having another masturbatory episode while the film is playing out but he then thinks better of it. Instead, Noah turns the television off and starts going through his wardrobe, thinking of what to wear for the day. As he begins this task, he suddenly becomes overwhelmed with a fatigue so great he has to lie down. This is fairly common for Noah, these sudden bouts of exhaustion; however, it is not helped in this instance by him having caught a view of the silver flight case, the one Smiley had delivered, the one with a bomb that could bring down an entire street inside of it, sitting there all shiny and new at the bottom of the closet, calling out to be opened. He lies across his king-sized hotel bed for about ten minutes, staring at the ceiling, all the while trying to think about as little as possible. But Noah is a massively famous pop star and thus never long without stimulation, whether he is looking for it or not. His phone starts to buzz. He immediately picks it up to examine who is calling. He smiles as he sees 'Eva' appear on his smartphone display.

'What do you want?' he says as drily as he can manage under the circumstances.

'That's no way to speak to an old friend, is it?'

Noah finds his loins stirring in response to Eva's sultry tones already. It was her voice that always got to him. That impossible-to-resist voice.

It was a delivery that could have convinced Noah to do almost anything.

'We were never friends,' Noah says.

'I was wondering if you'd had a chance to think over what we discussed last time we spoke.'

Noah's mind reels trying to recall what the hell Eva is talking about. All he can remember is a conversation in which she talked dirty to him while he masturbated. Actually, 'talked dirty' is somewhat of a misnomer; she spoke about nothing in particular and this was enough for him to jerk off to. *If only I could trap her voice, just her voice somehow and put it in a box. And that dismembered voice could read my mind and say back to me all of things I so long for it say, and I could listen to it whenever I felt lonely or horny and discard it afterwards with no messy feelings involved.* Her voice was the only thing about Eva he'd ever truly desired. Yes, she was also a good-looking woman. Not good-looking enough to overcome her unfortunate personality and sketchy hangers-on, but empirically attractive. Yet that voice, that voice, that voice . . .

'Refresh me?' Noah finally has to ask.

'You must remember my business proposal.'

Noah can't remember a business proposal of any sort, but he believes that she had presented him with one. It was probably what he had jerked off to.

'I'm afraid it's slipped my mind.'

'It was about my think tank.'

It then all comes rushing back to Noah, Eva's demented idea to start a Non-Governmental Organization based around her fucked-up, neo-Nazi bullshit. Worse, with her as its major intellectual driving force. She is angling for Noah to pay for it, something he wouldn't do even if he'd wanted to but certainly can't get involved with anyway given the fact that his entire livelihood rests on his squeaky-clean image. Funding a racist organisation would be obvious career suicide. *Although I am committing actual suicide today, so perhaps I should tell Eva she can have the money for the hell of it.* The thought of this makes Noah laugh out loud. Eva is instantly offended, her believing she is being mocked down the phone for her proposal.

'You don't need to be so cruel about it.'

Eva never seems to get that Noah isn't interested in her particularly, and he is definitely not interested in all of her Nazi shit or any of the people that come with it. Despite her constant, manipulative attempts to pry money out of Noah, she actually remains clueless about the effect of her voice on her intended rich and famous victim, and how that should be the key to her whole plan. It is this blind spot that has always caused her ploys to have Hastings fund her lifestyle fail so spectacularly.

'I'm hanging up in five seconds, Eva, so say your piece.'

'I love you, Noah.'

'No, you don't.'

And even though Noah knows she doesn't love him (Eva is incapable of the emotion in the first place) and he certainly does not love her or anything even close to such an emotion, these words sound so good coming from that luscious larynx that he starts to regret not having taped the phone call. He could have spent part of his last hour on Earth with that wondrous voice, saying the words he longed to hear for real, coming from a woman that he felt the same way about, imagining she sounded as good as Eva.

'Yes, I do. You know I do, Noah darling.'

Noah smiles. It shocked him every time they spoke that Eva never got it, the power she has over him, all to do with the sounds that emanated from her throat. If she told him that she loved him again, and then again, and then again, she would almost certainly have him. He'd submit, he'd break down, perhaps even give her the money for her hideous fascist think tank for real. Perhaps he would confess what he had planned to do that evening and her voice would stop him from carrying it through. This train of thought makes Noah laugh out loud again; the idea that a far-right terrorist could end up unintentionally saving the lives of the bourgeois children she would so love to kill herself was deliciously amusing in that instant.

Eva again takes the laughter to be directed at her and what she is suggesting, and as a result comes over all offended anew.

'Fine then, be that way, you ignorant little child! Go and sing your moronic, tuneless shit to the middle-class imbeciles who are willing to pay money for such a thing!'

And with that, the Nazi woman hangs up.

Noah first met Eva when she was going through a divorce from her third husband, an Austrian importer-exporter who was remarkably corpulent, had terrible breath, was desperate for Eva, but unfortunately for her, was also brilliant with his money. She thought she'd get a nice little packet from Gunther but in the end, she got extremely little. Although this was all still playing out when she met Noah at a reception for the LA mayor they were both attending (he as the guest of honour; she as the quasi-escort of a second-rate film producer), she could already sense that she was going to end up with not much out of her divorce from Gunther and thus, given her lack of employable skills, knew she'd have to find another rich gentleman to keep her in the lifestyle to which she had become accustomed. She chatted to the pop star on a whim, knowing she was shooting for the moon. The voice got to Noah immediately and they ended up sleeping together that evening.

Noah found Eva's political beliefs at first baffling and then amusing but didn't feel threatened by them until long after they had first met. Even when he had come into contact her awful Nazi friends, horrible pieces of work every last one of them, Noah didn't spend a great deal of time thinking about how warped Eva probably was. He was in a state of mind in which nothing could pierce his little bubble of fame and he took the whole thing as if it were a harmless cartoon. Until, that is, one night when he had Eva and some of her friends around his place for some stiff drinks and cocaine. This was right after Noah had abandoned his daily trip to the mosque on Sunset and was thus going through an uber-hedonistic phase. One of the Nazis started talking about how liberalism was weak because it always equalled appeasement, while communism at least was a pure ethos, if a totally false one, as it had direction and spirit. Liberalism on the other hand was all about simply letting every philosophy co-exist at once: an impossible state of affairs to continue indefinitely. Most of the big words the over-educated Nazi used flew over Noah's head and he found the increasingly strident tone boring, even with all the booze and coke flowing through his bloodstream. He made a light-hearted crack, something about how liberalism was the only reason he was tolerating the Nazi's bullshit in the first place, when his guest flipped out, grabbed Noah by the throat and pressed him into the wall. The fascist grabbed his windpipe so hard, in fact, that Noah almost blacked out straight off, even before the back of his head hit his own finely sanded surface (his carpenter was the best in Los Angeles). Eva got her friend to stop, mostly by hitting him in the arm hard enough so that he had to slap her away. Now free to speak and breathe again, Noah told them all to leave or he'd call the cops. He never saw any of the Nazis ever again – bar Eva, of course.

Yet the throat-crushing incident was what turned it for them too, and they began to quickly drift apart. Noah, having been physically assaulted, could no longer see Eva and her world as a harmless sideshow. Within weeks, he called Eva and told her they were through. However, he kept the copy of *Mein Kampf* she'd given him as a birthday present close by him wherever he travelled (for reasons he himself could never fathom). And of course, he answered her calls still, if only to hear her speak, regardless of the nonsensical shape the conversations took. The truth that he could hardly bring himself to face, never mind discuss with anyone else, was that Noah always felt uneducated and unsophisticated around Eva and her fascist friends. It was partly a north-south thing, all of the male Nazis being defectors from liberal, respectable East Coast households. The fact that Noah was extremely poorly educated and was an autodidact made things worse for him. He would often mispronounce a word or two, or throw a malapropism into a conversation, errors that the Nazis would never allow to pass without extreme censure. Despite being the rich, famous one, not to mention being the person who was not being heavily brainwashed by a totalitarian philosophy, Noah always felt he couldn't get the better of Eva and her friends in conversation, something that left deeper scars than the throat-squeezing did, ultimately.

Having eaten breakfast, beaten off to pornography, showered, had a pointless conversation with a female neo-Nazi and then finally picked out something to wear while resisting the urge to open or even fully look at Smiley's silver case, Noah can now finally leave the hotel for the first time that day. What motivates him to do so is catching sight of the Bible he'd left on top of the bedside table the previous night. Seeing it there makes him think of the Book of Revelations, which leads him to recall that this is, after all, his last day as a human being and time was going to waste. He looks outside to check the weather, the first time he has considered doing so since he had arisen a couple of hours previously. Grey overhead but no way was it going to rain anytime soon. He puts on a light jacket, one he'd picked up from some hipster store in the Village last time he was in New York, one that he can't recall having worn since he had purchased it.

Leaving his hotel, there is but one photographer, a rookie who is busy daydreaming and only gets to his feet and starts snapping after Noah has come and gone, thus getting only some unusable shots of the back of the pop star's head. Noah smiles to himself as he hears the tenderfoot curse himself, loudly as well, enough for him to get a 'watch yourself, kid' stare from the hotel's concierge, a man the photographer had no doubt paid way over the odds for information that turned out to be utterly worthless, a payment he is now going to struggle to explain to his employer.

Noah wanders westward down 63rd Street, although he has no consciousness of direction or destination. He is completely absorbed in thoughts of the evening ahead, mostly quasi-technical, remembering from Smiley the detail on how the explosive apparatus operated; which buttons you had to press to remove the safety features on it (of which there were, understandably, a fair few). Noah thinks back to all those years ago, when Smiley had shown him how to easily detonate a similar weapon in the heat of the moment and how it had to be set up in a particular, precise way in order to make this achievable. The more he ponders the details, the more Noah regrets having not first done a run-through with the bomb in his hotel room before he'd left on this journey to nowhere. He could be up there right now, quelling his own anxieties directly. He thinks about turning back and going to his room to do precisely this when he realizes he is directly across the road from Central Park. He then thinks he will take a stroll through the park for a while, clear his mind, and then turn his attention to business.

At the entrance to the park, a Hare Krishna distributing leaflets walks up to speak to Noah. The religious cultist is performing this task in a distinctly lacklustre, automated way; he'll hand someone one of his pieces of printed information, the passers-by will take it from him absentmindedly, and then walk with it for ten paces without looking at it once. They will then deposit it in the bin that stands about twenty paces away from the Hare Krishna's personal space. He catches sight of Noah as soon as the pop star enters the confines of Central Park and in doing so suddenly springs to life, the chance to try and reel in a big fish not to be resisted.

'Oh my God, are you really Noah Hastings? Of course you are, of course you are! I love all of your songs!'

'Aren't you guys banned from listening to anything but religious music?' Noah asks him, not unreasonably. The Hare Krishna chortles, the giggle of a hyperactive schoolgirl. Noah finds himself immediately annoyed at the leaflet-giver as a result of this.

'That's true. But you're a guilty pleasure.'

The Hare Krishna, beyond having an annoying laugh, is incredibly camp, perhaps the most outwardly effeminate man Hastings has ever personally come across; given he is a pop star who lives in Hollywood, that is truly saying something. *Probably gay and needed something stronger than his parents' brand of Christianity to keep him on the straight and narrow. Only in America would someone be so terrified of their own homosexuality that the thought of joining a religious cult noted for its extreme bizarreness was preferable than simply facing up to the truth. Only in America would it be preferable to tell your parents you had become a Hare Krishna rather than having to tell them you're gay.*

'I'll read your literature and give it some thought,' Noah says, grabbing one of the leaflets out of the sexuality-denying Krishna's hand, thinking this will allow him to move seamlessly onwards. But no – the camp Krishna holds out his arm to block Noah as he tries to move past, almost caressing the pop star in an inappropriate way as he does so.

'Not so fast, Monsieur Hastings. I want you to promise me you'll listen to what I have to say.'

A few people have started to stop and stare. Even in New York, a city where you can walk around for hours without even a hint of hassle as a celebrity, the sight of a world-famous pop star being man-handled by a religious nutcase is still worthy of a watch. Noah takes stock of the gathering crowd and knows he has to work fast.

'Get your hands off me, you fucked-up faggot,' Noah whispers in his ear. That does the trick. He lets go of Noah suddenly, as if he'd been punched in the stomach. He then watches Hastings walk off with a look of almost infinite sadness, his most vulnerable button having been pushed. He collects his thoughts enough to realize what he needs to do. Obviously, the man with the onion haircut needs to retaliate while Noah is still within earshot.

'That's right, Mr Hastings, just walk on by. On your way to a Bilderberg meeting, I have no doubt. Grease the palms that gave you your fame to start with, right? You have a nice day sucking up to the international banking conspiracy, sir.'

Noah grumbles to himself as he tries to shut the lunatic out. *All of these losers need to blame having never been successful on something external. It can't be that they don't have enough talent; no, there has to be some conspiracy working against them. It's why shitheads like him think it's worth their while to stand in Central Park and hand out flyers: there's no shortage of people who are disappointed with their lives and so there's always a chance that the Krishna crap is perfect for them.*

The real reason Noah had lashed out so fiercely at the Hare Krishna, in the pop star's partial defence, was that the gay religious devotee looked strangely like his father, shorn of hair, and anyone fitting that description tended to set Noah off. This is because Noah viscerally hates his father, still, even though the old man has been dead for a decade.

Noah's dad was a Baptist preacher who had a habit of pissing off the locals wherever he went (and he was never anywhere for long as a result) with a combination of his all-too-literal take on the Bible and his penchant for conning the locals out of their hard-earned cash. Even the most faith-ridden had problems with Abraham Hastings visiting their homes uninvited every Friday in order to make sure they weren't eating meat. With regard to the second problem, Abraham was in constant trouble with the law due to his proclivity towards low-level fraud, something which, as mentioned, provided an ongoing incentive towards a peripatetic lifestyle for the Hastings clan. Every few months saw another move, always to some new hellhole in the deep south. Little-frequented parts of Louisiana, Mississippi, Alabama, and Georgia all hosted the Hastings for brief stretches. That extensive travelling across the country as a young boy made Noah think that America went on for ever; that all of reality was somehow covered by the place, its people and its odd habits.

His genuine salvation was his own mind. He began reading independently when he was young, books from the library that he would sneak into the house. He started this habit partly out of an intellectual curiosity that could not be satiated by his father's the-Bible-as-reality teachings, nor the rather lame curriculums of the various schools he attended. But mostly it was borne from the fact that he had begun to have doubts about his parent's overriding worldview, and actually monotheism as a whole. Some of this mistrust stemmed from the rather transparent lies his father and mother would tell little Noah when they once again had to move on. After one particular move, it was because God had apparently told them personally that a tornado was going to destroy their house. Another time, that a whale was going to eat the town.

One day, Noah had an epiphany. It had been coming for some time, but this was the real breakthrough. It was all simple enough. He was sitting in a field of cotton, looking up at the sky. The clouds were moving swiftly above him as a storm gathered pace. Something about the movement of those clouds showed him definitively that there was no God. He saw clearly that the universe was a set of random events that the human need for order had tried to make sense of through an anthropomorphic deity. He raced home with a smile on his face, an intellectual itch he'd been trying to scratch for ages suddenly soothed.

Noah pretended that he believed in God for a long time after that little moment of clarity in any dealings with his parents, of course. His father was a preacher; a crooked one, but a man of the cloth nonetheless, and a devout one in his own warped fashion. His mother never caught on to her son's lack of belief, but his old man sniffed it out pretty quickly. After several months of faking it, thinking he'd pulled one over on his folks, a day arrived when his father told him that the two of them were going fishing the Saturday next. Noah instantly knew something was fishy beyond the obvious; he and his father had never previously been on any such rendezvous. Sure enough, as soon as they were in the boat, in the middle of the lake on what was unfortunately a miserable, rainy day, his father started in on him, creeping as he always did, beginning with authoritative calm, an approach Noah knew from experience was the harbinger of a mighty storm.

'I know, you know,' Abraham the preacher, son and father of Noahs, said in a relaxed voice to his little boy as the child sat and shivered in the drizzle.

'Know what?' Noah said, trying to play stupid, but even he could hear the panic in his own voice.

'That you been faking it the whole time on Sundays, at church. That you lost the faith somewhere along the way in the Almighty.'

Noah thought – for what would be the last time ever in his life – that he could reason with his father.

'You're right. I guess I sort of see through it all. I wish I could believe again, Pa. Sincerely I do. Once you see through something, that's it. You can never believe in the lie again.'

His father nodded, like he was genuinely absorbing what Noah was telling him, really listening, while gazing out at the lake in front of him. When Noah was finished talking, Abraham turned slowly towards his son. He smiled a little and then let out a light chuckle, one that seemed almost self-deprecating, not something Reverend Hastings tended to engage in often. This little mirth-filled phase from his father was short-lived; the next thing Noah knew he was underwater, or at least his upper half was. Not having been prepared for it, he found himself quickly panicking as he started to inhale water at what felt like a possibly life-ending rate. As he thrashed around, trying to get to the surface again, he then figured out that his father was holding on tightly to his legs and forcing him under. For a moment, Noah lost all heart as he thought his father had decided to murder him – and that given the man's superior strength he had no hope of surviving. However, the next moment saw him lifted out of the water and thrown back into the boat, landing hard on his head and his side. The pain caused by the landing was quickly shoved aside though, as Noah's only immediate concern was getting his breath back. Despite it feeling like he had taken a great deal of liquid into his lungs, he had in fact only inhaled a small amount that he was able to rather easily cough up. Once he had done this, he began sucking in great breaths of air, the drops of water still in his throat re-entering his windpipe, causing him to cough furiously.

Abraham meanwhile was sitting at the other end of the boat, studying his son the way a more cultured man would look at a painting in a museum. He was actually preparing for the next portion of saving his son's soul. When Noah had recovered enough to look up at his father, Abraham said to his offspring:

'When you went under there, did you think you were going to die?'

Noah nodded and then started to cry. He was only being truthful. For a brief moment near the end, before his father yanked him back up and into the boat, Noah thought his life might be over.

'And did you find that your faith in the Lord was suddenly there again?'

Noah was caught blind by this question. The whole concept of God hadn't even entered his thoughts during the whole traumatic episode up until this point. It was perhaps the furthest thing from his mind while he was physically inside the lake, close to drowning. Noah didn't have to say a thing; his father was able to read it all from his face. Before Noah could even think about protesting, or making something up, he found himself in the same position again, face and chest under the lake's surface. He was a little more prepared for it this time and didn't panic as much. His father was prepared for this eventuality however and kept Noah down there for a little longer than the first plunge. Soon, Noah was inhaling water again, this time more than he had before because the breaths he was taking were deeper. He was almost ready to pass out when his father brought him back up. In what counts as small mercies in such a situation, Abraham put his son down with a bit more subtlety the second time around.

Noah coughed and coughed and then threw up, scared enough of his father to still find the strength to pull his face overboard before vomiting (Abraham did not tolerate any sort of mess in his precious

boat, and despite Noah's lack of experience in the vessel, he understood his father enough to know this intuitively). He paused there
for a moment, facing the water, trying to figure out what to do. It
occurred to him that he could try diving in and swimming for it,
but this possibility he discounted almost immediately. His father was
a much better swimmer than he was, and once he'd tried that little
stunt, his father's rage could tip over into something uncontrollable
and then he actually might kill Noah. He did the only thing he
could do in the end, which was to turn around and face the music.

'You prayed that time, didn't you?' Abraham asked, a smile on his
face as he anticipated victory.

'Yes, I did. I prayed so hard when I was under that water, Pa,
you're right.'

But this tactic was doomed to failure. Abraham Hastings was a
born bullshitter if ever one walked the face of the Earth, and as such
was a genius at spotting when someone was being straight up with
him and when they were lying. It was the sole thing that had got
him through life to that point. Noah went to puke again, but this
was interrupted by finding himself face down in the water a third
time, his father holding him in once more. *Jesus, how does he move so
fast?* Noah asked himself. As he realized he had inadvertently evoked
a thought towards Jesus, albeit in vain, Noah laughed. Bad move
given his position. He soon found himself taking in water, sucking
it deep down into his lungs this time round. It wasn't long before he
was unconscious.

When he came to, his father was pumping his hands up and down
on his son's chest, looking terrified. When his son brought forth
from his mouth a torrent of water and began to cough, Abraham
actually cried in relief, the only time in his adult life he'd ever done
so. For a few terrifying moments he became convinced that he'd
overstepped the mark and killed his child inadvertently. Had this
occurred, he first would have felt the wrath of his wife, then the
penal system and then from the Lord above for the remainder of

eternity. Abraham reeled backwards as his son sat up, strangely filled with strength.

The father and son began to sail back to shore without another word having to be uttered. They didn't speak again for the rest of the car journey home either.

Persons magazine article on Amir Elahi, by David O'Willery – September 2021 issue

He has become one of the most notorious men in the United States of America. In the aftermath of the FBI's investigation into the June 16th Noah Hastings bombing at Madison Square Garden, Amir Elahi was briefly detained by the Bureau on suspicion of being an accomplice in the murders of ninety-one people. He was held briefly at the FBI's Los Angeles office before being released. The chief reason for him being placed under suspicion was that he flew from Los Angeles to New York on the morning of June 16th, the day of the MSG bombing, met with Noah Hastings briefly at the pop star's hotel and then almost immediately returned to JFK and got on the next flight back to Los Angeles.

'Mr Hastings wandered into my mosque thirty-eight months ago. I approached him and we began to speak about his life,' Mr Elahi told me when I came to California to speak with him at his home. 'He seemed to me to be searching for something. I proposed to him that perhaps Islam could fill this void inside. This was something he seemed open to at the time of our first few meetings.'

Amir Elahi lives alone, as he has done since he arrived in America sixteen years ago having emigrated from Pakistan. I asked him if he had ever thought of getting married.

'Every day,' he told me with a slightly pained smile. 'But I never found a woman devout enough for me. In California, such things are in short supply.'

Mr Elahi is a charming man. This isn't something I had expected. His house is spartan but neat. It is clearly an ageing bachelor's residence, one occupied by a man with too much time on his hands. Despite having been released by the FBI with no charge – he was also brought in for questioning several further times over the summer months – the imam has suffered unwanted attention from both the press and the public.

'It is a rare day I am not approached by someone. Either a reporter or a random stranger who wishes to take issue with me on the basis of what has been printed.'

I ask him if he has ever been threatened by violence in such a situation.

'Rarely, but it does happen on occasion. I have been lucky so far, I think.'

We wandered out into his backyard. Like the house it sits behind, it is small, tidy and strangely welcoming. Having suggested we go outside for some fresh air, I questioned Mr Elahi about Noah Hastings' conversion to Islam.

'One misconception that needs clarifying right now is that Mr Hastings at no point became a Muslim, at least when I knew him. The path to Islam is clear and easy, but it is one that, despite a great deal of discussion between he and I on the subject, Mr Hastings never took. At least when I knew him, I'd like to once again stress. Subsequent to our friendship ceasing, he may have become a Muslim, I do not know.'

Mr Elahi then pauses to reflect further upon his time in Noah Hastings' company.

'For eleven weeks, Mr Hastings came to the mosque almost every single day. It was an intense time, one in which he became a sort of student of mine. He wanted to know everything he could about Islam. About the faith, the way of life. He also wanted to know more about life in Islamic countries. I was happy to share this information with such an eager listener. I tried to push him, lightly, to convert to Islam, but this he always refused. He said that such a thing was a large commitment, one that he did not want to enter

74

into before being completely sure. Then he stopped coming to the mosque altogether, just like that. I went from seeing him, as I say, most days, to never seeing him at all.'

I was warming up to the big questions I had come to ask. The ones regarding his brief trip to New York City on June 16th. I first questioned him about his mosque and his other less famous parishioners. Mr Elahi lit up at the mention of this, clearly the centre of his everything. He sounded like an elderly Christian minister as he answered me, regaling a stranger with tales of the latest fundraising lunch mishap and a question about God from a small child who attends with his parents nudging. When I brought up New York, however, all of the joy drained from his face instantly. Back was the gaze I met at his front door when I had first arrived. Guarded, apprehensive, resigned, and yet still somehow friendly and inviting underneath it all.

'Mr Hastings gave me a phone call on the evening of June fifteenth. He told me then that he needed to see me as soon as possible. At this point I had not spoken to him for three years, bear this in mind. He told me that I needed to get on a flight to New York and meet with him at his hotel room. I quickly reminded Mr Hastings that I was not a man of extravagant means like he was and could not simply afford to pay for a flight to New York, just like that. He said he would buy me a plane ticket and did so while we were on the phone with each other, a flight leaving early the following morning. I accepted his offer and came to New York, something I now deeply regret.

'I had no idea what was going to happen and had I known, I would never have come, not in a thousand years. I have to confess that a large portion of my motivation for dropping everything and getting on that flight across the country was down to Mr Hastings', shall we call it, popularity. It was one of the reasons, I also should confess right now, that I was so eager to convert him during the eleven weeks he was my pupil. I thought that if a major figure amongst the children of America could become a Muslim, this would help the way that so many Americans perceive Islam. Sadly, the exact opposite of what I had hoped would take place has done so, with Islam more vilified in America than ever before.'

At this point, we alighted in front of a small allotment of vegetables that sits at the back of Mr Elahi's backyard. He frowned a little as he examined some of his lettuces, telling me as he picked some wilted leaves off of one of them that they don't grow properly in southern California, the poor vegetables. I asked him why he keeps trying to grow them if that is the case. He simply chuckled and asked me to ask him the next question on my list. It was his subtle way of telling me that his hospitality was reaching its limit. I asked him straight up what he and Noah Hastings discussed when they met in New York City the day of the bombing.

'Not much. As I said, it was a disappointing conversation from my perspective. Mr Hastings appeared to be a little intoxicated when I arrived. I had never seen him like this before and did not like it. When he came to the mosque, he was always sober and respectful. When I saw him in New York, he was flippant and yet angry at one and the same time. I got the general sense that he had forgotten all about inviting me to come see him, possibly because he had been drinking alcohol the previous evening when he had done so, and now that I was there in front of him, he simply took the opportunity to make light of me and my faith.'

Mr Elahi looked down at the ground as he recounted the next portion of his story. It was the one time he seemed shameful.

'He called me disrespectful names and said that I was a fool for following an "invisible man". He then said that faith itself was a stupid thing and that Islam was no different than the Christianity he had rejected in his youth. Then he began to make fun of my diet.'

The lettuces? I asked him, trying to lighten the mood. It worked. Mr Elahi's smile was back. He said to me then that Noah Hastings had never had a kind word about curry, something that made me like the deceased pop star even less than I did already. Mr Elahi then told me about why he left so quickly to get back to LA the same day as arriving.

'I had only come because Mr Hastings had requested I come to New York to see him and was willing to pay for me to do so. My conversation with him was brief and upsetting and made me wish to be back here in my home as soon as possible.'

I asked him where he was when he found out about the bombing.

'I was here at home. It was the following morning. I turned on the television and, of course, it was everywhere. I instantly felt sick to my stomach because, you know, I had seen him only a few hours before it had happened. Your mind reels in that situation, wondering if there was some sign you should have picked up on. Something that was there that could have told you what was going on in his mind.'

Relating his experiences of June 15th,16th and 17th to me was visibly emotionally draining for Mr Elahi. I suggested to him at this point that we go back inside. He nodded and I followed in behind him.

Before I departed, Mr Elahi delivered his final thoughts on Noah Hastings.

'As I said, Mr Hastings was not a Muslim, at least when we were acquainted. Although I cannot confirm this for certain, I do not believe that Mr Hastings became a Muslim subsequent to our time together as associates and as such I do not believe that what motivated Mr Hastings to take his life and the lives of the others that night was Islam or any form of Muslim faith.'

After he finished this speech, I wanted to ask him about his time growing up in Quetta. There are various pictures of him as a young man dotted around his living room, usually ones featuring a young Amir dressed in his cricket whites. I wanted to ask about his sporting youth, but I could tell he had told me all that was available for him to say that day.

On the journey back to New York – the same one Mr Elahi had made himself on June 16th – I considered everything the imam had told me about his one-time prospective student. What is hard to convey in a magazine article is how convincing the man was in person. I found it hard to disregard anything he said, even when his story contradicted the official one by a wide margin. As I munched a leaf of lettuce from Mr Elahi's garden I had managed to sneak through airport security, I found myself more puzzled about Noah Hastings than ever before.

'Syria and the Noah Hastings suicide', an article by James Adams, foreign correspondent for the *New York Sentinel*, September 23rd, 2021

While sitting in certain quarters of Damascus, one can almost forget that there is a still a war going on nearby. Although the tourist trade died a decade ago when the civil war began, the restaurants still do a decent trade; the tea stalls are still lively and the shops seem to keep going, somehow or other. Only when one hears a bomb go off somewhere in the near distance, all of the faces suddenly stirred back into a world of mortal fear, trying to guess from the sound how close the explosion was and thus how far away an invading army might be, does the war rear its ugly head again into one's consciousness. The fear of Sunni insurgents storming Damascus is for now a remote fear. Yet the fear of it happening someday never disappears altogether.

The Noah Hastings incident at Madison Square Garden this past summer has had an effect on America that is hard to exaggerate. Meanwhile, how it is perceived in the Middle East and Syria in particular is complex.

'I heard that this man was maybe a martyr, so I download some of his music. But I only listen to a little bit,' a contact of mine who is an Islamic Fighters for a Caliphate member told me. 'The lyrics are decadent, nothing to do with Islam at all. It is clear to me that this singer was an infidel.'

Many representatives from the newly formed Sunni–Coalition I have spoken with about Noah Hastings and the events of June 16th feel that the American government has completely manufactured the connection between the bombing and Islam.

'They want an excuse to get further involved in the Middle East situation. They have tried everything to get the American people scared about the repercussions of this war on their own country and possibly on Israel, but nothing so far has worked,' said Abel Fatah, a Sunni-Coalition corporal. 'Then this singer kills himself and a bunch of his followers and they think, now is our opportunity. The Americans realized they made a mistake all those years ago when they could have stopped this whole war almost at its birth. Now they want to intervene further but know the American public would not stand for such a thing – beyond protecting Israel, if that becomes necessary.'

It comes as no surprise that the Noah Hastings bombing is spoken about in the same breath as American military involvement in the burgeoning Sunni-Shia war in Syria given that is the lens through which everything is seen here at present. Furthermore, speaking about the death of an American pop singer while somehow bringing Israel into the equation is par for the course in this part of the world.

'Israel has been quiet since they downed those Syrian fighter jets in the summer. They think they have no involvement in this affair of the Arabs, or that perhaps the situation even works to their advantage as Shia and Sunni begin to tear themselves apart. I can tell you this: the Israelis have got themselves into a false sense of security. We are all waiting for the right moment to pounce.'

That was a quote, off the record, from someone high enough up in the military command of one of the principle agitator countries in the Sunni-Shia War. The war will be coming to Israel at some point relatively soon unless America does something about it first.

It is remarkable to watch a war on the scale of the one in the Middle East currently and remind oneself that the American government has had what amounts to an uncharacteristically tiny dabble in the whole conflict.

'The Americans could stop everything now if they wished. They would fall in behind the Saudis even further and thus end the Shia bid for dominance in large portions of the Arab world,' Dr Ruhani, a professor of Arab Studies at the University of Cairo, told me. 'But what scares the Americans is the Israel problem. They know they could be building up an army to end the Sunni-Shia War that would then turn around and attempt to destroy Israel. So, they stand back, choosing not to get too heavily committed militarily. By doing so, I believe they are simply storing up problems for their own interests in the region – including Israel.'

One can speculate that perhaps the misadventures of the early twenty-first century in Afghanistan and Iraq have soured Americans against military intervention. Let us recall that the current president ran explicitly on a ticket of no escalation of American military involvement in the Middle East. I believe that given American military escapades in the Middle East in decades past has directly led to the current war in the region taking place, one should reflect the sadness of America's current position in this horrible conflict.

Here in Damascus, the way that the normalcy of war has become a way of life continues to stagger those from the outside, including even myself, people here to cover the horror who mostly find warm Syrian faces, hookah on demand, and the best coffee in the world. Some days, like I said at the beginning, you could almost forget that one of the worst wars in the history of the world is taking place not so far away. Almost.

'Acting Like Black Sabbath', a piece in the October 2021 edition of *Rocking Teen Combo* magazine, by Jolo Martins

When I was a teenager, a group of friends and I would often assemble at one of the gang's older brother's shitty apartment (I use the descriptive word here literally – the carpet had been defiled so much by the dog you never dared remove your shoes), a lair in which we would proceed to smoke hashish and listen to Black Sabbath's *We Sold Our Souls for Rock and Roll*. Diggy's brother (my friend wasn't actually called Diggy. I'm giving him a pseudonym for reasons which will soon become clear) had this as his only compact disc, otherwise I think we would have rotated the musical selection once in a while (although there is obviously no way to test this theory). We did hashish hot knives after which we would lounge on the dingy couch listening to Tony Iommi, Geezer Butler, Bill Ward and Ozzy Osbourne navigate the grooves of the universe.

Every time before we started smoking up, we'd draw straws to see who had to get up off of the couch and press the 'next track' button on the CD player (the remote had long since vanished in some previous stoned haze) to the next number once 'Changes' had made its unwanted appearance. For those of you who are unaware of this song, it is a piano ballad unlike anything else in Black Sabbath's oeuvre. Over time, the song has grown on me, but as a dope-smoking teen I loathed it. We all did, especially as 'Sweet Leaf', the group's ode to cannabis, was the next track along.

On one particular afternoon, Diggy drew the shortest straw. He proceeded to complain that it was unfair that he should have to perform this task as he was the one providing the venue, through his brother, for us to all get together, smoke dope and listen to Sabbath in the first place. We ganged up on him, telling Diggy that if he felt he deserved an exemption from the process he should have said so before participating (it should be noted here that of the six-fold gang there that day, three of them went on to become highly paid defence lawyers). He was pissed off about it, but reluctantly agreed when he could see that no hashish consumption was going to begin until he stopped his bitching.

Everything was going along smooth as could be when 'Fairies Wear Boots' faded out and we all braced ourselves for the horror of those opening piano chords. Stares began to accumulate in Diggy's direction. He coped with this as I thought he might at the outset: he pretended he was too stoned to know what was going on. As 'Changes' began, so too did the outright complaining and cajoling of Diggy to get up and do his duty.

'Give me a second,' he said like a little boy being unduly woken from his afternoon nap. Then the kicking began as one of our bunch, the ever-excitable Bunny (that's not his real name either, but you all probably figured that out yourselves) began to flail his legs at Diggy. This did the trick (mostly by knocking Diggy off his brother's couch) in terms of getting the man who had drawn the shortest straw to take his short walk towards the CD player. Yet instead of pressing the correct button, Diggy (by accident, he later claimed, although no one believed him) hit the 'loop' button, meaning he had technically made 'Changes' go on for the rest of time. The shouts got louder and angrier the more that Diggy hit random buttons in an attempt to reverse what he'd done, all to no avail. We were halfway through the last verse before someone finally figured out that we could simply turn the CD player off and on again.

I bring this all up because where we have ended up with the whole Noah Hastings thing reminds me a lot of Diggy, 'Changes' and drawing the shortest straw. Just over three months ago, the FBI made a provocative announcement to the press, one declaring that Noah Hastings had been motivated by his belief in Islam in carrying out the bombing of June 16th and that their investigation into the matter would proceed on that basis. And in the ensuing three months, nothing has happened. Nothing whatsoever. There has been one further announcement from the FBI, which offered no news on where the investigation is at present. No arrests have been made. The FBI are like Diggy: sitting on the couch as everyone screams at them, angry that the commitment they made to move the music along is being ignored. It made me wonder this week how they had enough time on their hands to harass NWA in the late 1980s but now can't seem to come up with a single lead on what is the crime of the century. You also fear that once they do finally do whatever it is they are going to end up doing, it will be something that will be the equivalent of making the worst Black Sabbath song go on for ever and ever in a loop.

Do you want to hear about something even more depressing? This is the transcript from a recent conversation I had with my teen-aged son:

'Do you guys ever listen to Sabbath?'

'It's the twenty-first century, Dad. We listen to Noah Hastings.'

'But Noah Hastings is cheesy pop shit. He's not even rock and roll.'

'Yeah, but that stunt he pulled at Madison Square Garden was pretty rock and roll.'

'Killing yourself in the name of religious fundamentalism is rock and roll now?'

'That Islam line is bo-shita (*note: without wishing to sound like an old man, slang is going through a lousy phase, isn't it?*). Noah killed himself for rock and roll.'

'Why don't you all go for it and listen to One Direction?' I said mockingly. My son scrunched up his face and looked at me like I'd just let a horrible fart rip.

'Dad, they totally suck. Plus, they are, like, totally old school.'

I have no idea how ubiquitous this approach to Noah Hastings is amongst our teenagers. I do find it slightly scary that anodyne pop music can be reinvented as edgy rock and roll simply by means of killing ninety-one people, however lightly spread that belief happens to be. In my son's case, it seems to stem from an inherent and deeply felt distrust of what the 'American establishment' has to say about anything, so he has a tendency to automatically believe the reverse of whatever the White House/FBI/state police apparatus (despite those various pillars of the establishment not exactly agreeing with one another these days) might tell him to think. I also find the notion that One Direction are 'old school' terrifying in the extreme, but that's just me getting old.

Should I be worried about the fact that Noah Hastings is being embraced as some sort of rock and roll legend for what is a horribly cowardly and malicious act? One more nail in the coffin of this once great nation? Am I now most definitely sounding middle aged? I'm more worried about the musical implications, frankly. Noah Hastings' body of work is truly terrible – possibly the most boring, safe, moronic poop ever peddled by the now moribund music industry since its inception. Hastings should have been sentenced to life imprisonment for his cover version of 'Get Ur Freak On' alone (I was tempted to say 'put to death' instead of recommending the life sentence but thought that would probably be considered in bad taste. Plus, I'm anti-capital punishment and like to remain consistent whenever possible).

What I probably need to do is tell my son and his friends to listen to tunes one day at our place. Once I have them in my own lair, I will lock them in a room and force them to sit through *We Sold Our Souls for Rock and Roll* in its entirety. Even – and perhaps especially – 'Changes'. As for the FBI, well, not even rock and roll can save their souls. Come up with something – anything – will you, guys?

85

'Voices of dissent within the FBI reveal an investigation in crisis', Nina Hargreaves, *Washington Telegraph*, October 25th, 2021

The FBI has officially confirmed today that they have arrested Amir Elahi, the Los Angeles based imam, on ninety-one counts of conspiracy to commit murder in the first degree. Mr Elahi had been questioned by the Bureau in the immediate aftermath of the Noah Hastings bombing in June, yet at the time was released without charge. The FBI have not released any other information regarding Mr Elahi's involvement in the bombing other than to confirm that he has been arrested in connection with the incident.

This is the first arrest of the FBI's hopelessly drawn-out investigation into the Noah Hastings related June 16th incident. One arrest in four months is a small return for what has been a massive investigation, both in terms of scope and resources. While the arrest of Mr Elahi points outwardly to a breakthrough in the case, behind the scenes sources at the FBI have informed me otherwise.

'It looks like the central team are missing a smoking gun evidence-wise in terms of Elahi,' said one agent who has been working on and off on the Hastings investigation since it started. 'There doesn't seem to be anything more substantial on him than when they brought him in back in June. I think they've cuffed him to show they were getting somewhere with the whole thing, in all honesty. They figure they "Guantanamo" the guy and maybe they catch a break.'

Mistakes were made in the Hastings investigation right from the start, other off-the-record Bureau sources tell me, not least of which was the press announcement on June 22nd mentioning a connection between radical Islam and the bombing.

'Huge tactical error, that was,' another FBI source said. 'All they had back then was the stuff from the dressing room and the basic details of the Elahi connection. There was a group of investigators that were the core team who figured that the Islamic stuff was going to come flying out of the woodwork. They wanted to put out the Islamic connection to the public because they figured it would help loosen the screws, you know, like people would get scared and run, or witnesses would come forward. They were shocked when they put out the press release and nothing happened.'

The number of Bureau agents who clearly feel that the case has been mishandled and that the work of the Bureau has thus been compromised in an unprecedented way is genuinely staggering.

'Hands down, the worst investigation I've ever seen in twenty years with the Bureau,' the most senior source I spoke with from the FBI said to me. 'It would have to be judged as poor even by the standards of a local police investigation in a small town, never mind by the FBI. Really amateur stuff.'

The source seemed remarkably upset as he told me this, almost personally let down. I asked him why he thought the investigation had been so badly handled, in his opinion.

'I have no idea. I wish I knew. It's baffling. It may be one for the conspiracy theorists.'

At a time when America is facing unprecedented criminal justice issues as well as a lack of faith in the FBI from the White House itself, to hear that the federal police force is seemingly falling apart is a terrifying thought. If the FBI is at the point of arresting people simply to try and demonstrate they are doing something, like a local cop shop in some lousy 1980s TV show, not to mention then applying the 'Guantanamo' treatment to the suspects under detention, this constitutes a major crisis in our country on several levels.

It should be noted that even the release of a punchy media notice such as the one the Bureau let loose on June 22nd would have been far from normal FBI practice even five years previously. The national press office of the Bureau used to do a hard line in extremely turgid articles to the media, with extra care taken to give forth as little information as was absolutely necessary. To have essentially announced to America that Noah Hastings was an Islamist, particularly before any hard evidence had emerged, demonstrates either a sharp decline in National Press Office efficiency, or some sort of ideological change in direction at the top of the Bureau which in itself has gone directly unannounced.

I asked the FBI for an official response to the allegations presented in this article by internal sources. They declined to comment – in an official capacity anyhow. I will do the National Press Office the courtesy of not repeating what was said to me off the record.

'Mr Smiley can read the future', by Bob Anonymous, from the weekly periodical, *The Grassy Knoll* (sold by direct enquiry to the publisher only), November 12th, 2021 edition

We all know that the Noah Hastings suicide bombing was not motivated by Islam, in the same way we know that the bringing down of the World Trade Centre in 2001 was a crime perpetrated by the George W. Bush administration directly. I know I'm stating the obvious here but sometimes that becomes necessary. If the Islam story is a sham (and it obviously is), then why did Noah Hastings kill himself and all those fans in New York? The explanation put forward by some in the liberal lamestream press, the few that are willing to accept that perhaps Islam was not to blame, can only go as far as to postulate that it was a random act of violence. What happened on June 16th of this year was no accident: again, I know I don't even need to tell you people that, I'm just stating it for the record. No, it was a mass web of deceit involving the usual culprits: the CIA, the Pentagon, the Zionist establishment, the Bilderberg Group. But to add to this list are some unfamiliar names as well, such as John K. Smiley.

Mr Smiley is a Baptist preacher. Or at least he was one for several decades until he was excommunicated from most of the parishes in the south and found he couldn't carry on milking one church after the next. Did I mention that John K. Smiley is a con man? And that John K. Smiley is not his real name but a fake one he uses to use people? His real name is Jeremiah Samson and he was born somewhere in Louisiana in the 1970s. In the early part of this century, right after the events of September 11th, 2001 (coincidence?), Smiley aka Samson was arrested in Arkansas for a scam that crossed state lines. This meant he had to be tried FEDERALLY, which is big deal as all of you know. But the CIA stepped in and offered Smiley a deal: he tells them where the Manchu medal is hidden and not only does he walk a free man, they will train him up as a CIA operative. Job done for Mr Smiley, then.

The Manchu medal, I should explain for those who are not frequent readers, is a magical amulet which can predict the future. It was left here by the original Chinese settlers of North America, the ones who ran what some donuts refer to as 'Atlantis', but was actually a continuation of the Zing dynasty (this is why Native Americans look so Chinese). They fled when the Manchu medal told them of the arrival of the *Mayflower* from England, knowing the Puritans would have eaten them for breakfast, literally. But they left behind the medal that saved them, sailing to conquer Africa (at which they failed miserably, the Zulus destroying all trace of them – see the May 10th, 2017 edition for my article entitled 'The Manchu Medal and the Puritans: a first Thanksgiving to remember' which offers more detail on this for those interested). No one knows what happened to it. That is until Smiley discovered it sometime in the late 1990s, working one of his rare scams on the Eastern Seaboard (he tends to stick to the south). It was hidden in Baltimore Harbor, where Smiley had gone to find some pearls that someone had apparently let fall overboard one of the ships that had come in and out of Maryland Bay. He didn't find those pearls. He found a whole lot more. He found magic.

So, if Smiley had a medal that could read the future, how was it that he couldn't see the feds coming in Arkansas? Smiley refused to use the medal's powers, sighting his own belief in the Baptist faith. It was an occult item, something he had sworn never to engage with. Instead he buried the medal, knowing it would come in handy someday. And boy did it ever, particularly when he emerged from the CIA training base in Area 51, New Mexico practically some sort of ninja, knowing not just the most up-to-date intelligence-gathering techniques, but also everything the aliens have taught us that the government is currently sitting on.

So fine, now we know about John K. Smiley and his awesome skills: but how did he meet Noah Hastings and how did he then convince a multi-millionaire pop singer to blow himself up in front of thousands of fans? The answer is simple: bacon.

Noah Hastings had one fatal flaw (one that proves he wasn't a Muslim, incidentally) and that is his love of all pig-related food products. It is well known amongst CIA operatives (of whom I have known more than a few in my time) that Smiley can get his hands on unlimited quantities of any pig meat going as a result of a scam he pulled off in the late 1980s in Nebraska. Smiley promised Hastings as much bacon as he could eat if he could find someone who could do a passable impression of the pop idol for a few songs who was willing to blow himself up. Noah Hastings found such a man: Jeke De Willikers, a mentally retarded man from Illinois. A mug. A rube. Hastings got this man, this flaming retard, to take the hit. Now the former singer sits somewhere in Nebraska, unbothered by the world, eating swine flesh all the live long day.

Meanwhile, we're told he did it all for Allah, a deity that loathes pig eaters. Oh, isn't the world is full of terrible ironies. But you, the faithful, knew that already too.

June 16th, part three ('I want to switch seats')

Noah doesn't look back at the Hare Krishna after said religious devotee in Central Park starts to yell derogatory things at the pop star, and thus Noah does not see the cultist burst into hysterical tears once Noah is out of earshot. At this point, all Noah can focus on, once again, is how he should have examined the contents of the silver flight case and figured out how the bomb worked before he left the hotel room. He is chastising himself, internally, over and over again, while simultaneously attempting to get his mind off the topic and onto something else altogether, anything else.

'You're thinking about how you should have figured out how it all worked before you left the hotel, ain't ya?'

Hearing the voice directly behind his shoulder say these words turns Noah's flesh to ice. His stomach begins to hurt in a way it hadn't since the last time he had been face to face with the man who was part nemesis, part saviour, all pain in the ass. Noah swallows hard, knowing a strange and possibly painful conversation is inevitable. He stops dead and spins around to face the man, John K. Smiley, the devil on his shoulder, having decided the right tactic is to go in hard.

'How long have you been following me?'

'Since you left the hotel, jackass. I was in the coffee shop across the street. Saw that photographer fuck up like he did, whoa nelly, that was entertainment.'

'What do you want, John?'

Smiley spreads his arms and screws his face into a mask of mocked offence.

'A thank you would be nice. Isn't it all you hoped it would be after all? Of course, I say that knowing you have no goddamn idea because you haven't had the balls to even open the case and look at it yet, have ya.'

Smiley always knew. Somehow, he could always read Noah perfectly, better than Noah could read himself.

'What of it? It is a large-scale explosive device, John. Perhaps I didn't want to blow up half the hotel.'

'You want to save yourself for the kiddies, I get it. Not as good a story is it? "Moron pop singer accidentally blows himself and a bunch of rich assholes up". Yeah, not so good, I get it.'

'I'm sure that's exactly what the headlines would read like, yes.'

'Do you want my help or don't ya?'

Noah takes a deep breath and considers his options. No, of course he doesn't want Smiley hanging around for the rest of the day, which is what accepting his help on the ins and outs of the weapon will probably mean. Noah considers the horror of spending his last day on Earth with John K. Smiley and shudders. He then convinces himself he doesn't need the explosives guru; he will remember himself when the time comes how everything works. Noah's visual memory is excellent and it wasn't all that long ago that Smiley had last shown him the ropes. He feels like once he sits down with the bomb there in front of him, it will all come back to him. Noah takes a deep breath, working up his courage.

'Fuck off, John. I got what I needed from you and I don't wish to see you ever again. Thanks for everything.'

Smiley surveys the face of his young former amanuensis. He understands at once that Noah isn't messing around; that he means it. At least for the time being.

'Your wish is my command, oh mighty pop Lord.'

'And stop following me!'

'Ten four.'

As Smiley slopes off into another part of Central Park, Noah knows he hasn't seen the last of the crazy old preacher. He feels it in his bones. *Smiley will show up again, like the ghost of Christmas Future. I'll turn around at some point in the day and there he'll be.*

Noah starts to drift towards the Lennon memorial, close to where the Park meets the Upper West Side. He goes there every time he comes to New York City, no matter what he has on. He'd actually made a conscious decision not to go there this time around, on what was to be his last ever visit to the city he was about to die in; he found himself going there unconsciously anyhow.

Noah is staring at the monument to the assassinated Beatle when he gets the distinct feeling he's being watched. Sure enough, as soon as he looks around to either dispel or verify this hunch, he spots a nun who is standing about twenty metres away who is staring at him intensely; gawking and pointing at Noah like he's a zoo animal. In the next moment after Noah has clocked her, the nun approaches him, looking at nothing but Noah the whole time, almost knocking down a stray toddler along the path to the singing sensation's personal space she is now invading.

'Are you . . . ?'

'That's me.'

She blushes like a teenager in heat.

'Mr Hastings, can I just say I'm such a big fan of not only your music, but of the example you set for our young people.'

Noah struggles to maintain a straight face. What was it in his sexual innuendo-strewn pop career that this bride of Jesus had found so much in to admire? What particular lyric that had strayed from his mouth did she genuinely think communicated something useful to the youth of today?

'You don't say,' he manages to get out in at least a semi-non-sarcastic tone of voice.

'I think you're a lot like the man we're both here to pay our respects to today. I refer, of course, to the late, great John Lennon.'

Noah had been compared to many, far and wide, during his pop career, but never a Beatle and certainly not Lennon. He tries to digest the comparison but can't; it feels totally meaningless to him. The nun might as well have compared him to Gandhi or Simon Bolivar. Thus, he says nothing whatsoever in response. Noah hopes she'll get the hint and move on. The nun continues on anyhow.

'Like Mr Lennon, you are an ambassador for peace.'

Noah simply cannot face this comment without laughing, particularly given what he has sitting in his hotel room closet. The nun looks on horrified as Noah gives himself completely up to the moment, laughing so hard he ends up struggling for breath. *Perhaps this nun's comment is going to kill me before I get the chance to do it myself.* She starts to back away from the pop star as if he were deranged. The nun is so freaked out by the incident, in fact, that she wanders right out of the Park itself, seemingly without thought to where she's headed next. Noah watches her go for about half a minute, a sort of Zen experience as he begins to laugh less and less, seeing the nun wander west on 72nd Street totally aimlessly with a gormless expression oppressing her face. He then wanders back over to the circle which comprises the main monument to the ex-Beatle, the member of the group who had told America his band were bigger than Jesus. As he stares mock-ponderously at the Lennon monument, he reminisces for the first time about the flight from Los Angeles to New York made the previous day, the one during which he had made the decision to blow himself up on stage at Madison Square Garden tonight.

As he sat in the business class lounge of LAX, sipping the lime margarita he'd ordered against his better judgement – he had still been in the midst of an alcohol-free kick up until that drink – Noah felt depressed. He was slightly dreading the world tour he would soon embark on, one taking in Australia. He hated going to Oceania for any reason. The flight was ass-numbingly long and when you got there the fans were nuts; properly unhinged, and he'd had a few close scrapes every time he'd been down under. There had even been an assassination attempt in Sydney last time out; not some kid trying to shoot him with a .22 style bullshit, but some proper ninja stuff involving two kids with hacked security information and military grade weapons. Unfortunately, they loved him in Oz more than pretty much anywhere on Earth else except for China (*thank Christ I'm not playing there this year*). He played to 100,000-seat sports stadiums down there as opposed to the hockey arena shit he did in America where the venues were always three-quarters full (at best), and the theatres he struggled to fill these days when he infrequently toured Europe.

'Flight 912 to JFK now boarding for business-class passengers only,' came the announcement over the PA system. Noah hauled himself up, finished his drink and sauntered on board. He did this without informing Jules or the rest of the entourage, who then tried to get to Noah before he disappeared onto the plane. This was Noah's intention – ditching Jules without a word, and it was a goal he succeeded in achieving. His cronies got special dispensation to sit in the business-class lounge despite the fact that they all flew economy. This was a special arrangement, predicated on account of Noah having been a spokesperson for that particular airline for a spell.

'Champagne, sir?' asked the stewardess that Noah only belatedly noticed was rather attractive as she leaned over to enquire about his alcohol requirements. *Why the hell not?* Having consumed that lime margarita, Noah wanted to keep the party rolling.

'Yes, please.'

He turned around to check out the stewardess' behind as she departed, Noah now with champagne flute in hand. *Less impressive from the back. Sort of a boy's butt, unfortunately.* He turned to face forward again. As he did so, he realized he was coincidentally facing Mecca, something some quick calculations based on a few points of external data told him (crucially, an older man a few rows ahead and to the right was looking at a compass). He bent his head down and thought about saying a Salat as a bit of an homage to a retro version of himself. As he was considering doing this for old times' sake he found two people, a man and a woman, both in their early thirties, hovering in front of him, something which broke his train of thought.

'Sorry,' the man said offhandedly as he gestured with his coat-encumbered arm towards the window seat, clearly indicating that was where he wanted to go if Noah could politely facilitate this by getting up and removing himself from the way. Noah begrudgingly put his legs up to his knees and waved them through. The man made a face and reluctantly squeezed past Noah into the window seat, clearly annoyed that Noah hadn't got up and properly let him in. The woman did the same, squeezing into the middle seat, only as she did so offered Noah a brusque 'thanks!', said in such a way the sarcasm of the one-word comment could not be misconstrued. Noah continued staring ahead of himself during this interlude, through his Ray-Bans, trying to look unaffected. He then closed his eyes and was set to embark on his semi-ironic, alcohol-bathed prayer once more when the sound of children entered his ears. He opened his eyes to see two kids, a boy and a girl, the boy about eight years of age and the girl around ten, bounce past him and into the two seats in the row directly in front of him.

'You have to be quiet, okay? This is business class and people here expect good behaviour,' the woman beside Noah said to both of whom seemed at this stage to be her biological children. The kids were well-behaved and did as the woman instructed, settling down to read the fairly advanced fiction they had brought on board with them. He couldn't see what the girl was reading, but Noah noted the boy was reading a Roberto Bolaño book. Noah felt a twinge of disgust. *These rich assholes and the way that they indoctrinate their children with their leftie, foreign intellectual bullshit.* Noah had never read any Bolaño, but a review of the guy's work that he'd scanned while on a flight years ago had told him all he needed to know.

Unless there is a solid financial reason to do otherwise, Noah always flies in solitude up in business class while his underlings travel on the same flight in economy. They are only allowed to tag along on the same plane to conform to the 'never alone in public' rule, as well as in case he might need anything in an emergency-type situation. Noah and Murray never fly on the same airplane anymore; not since 2016, when they actually got into a physical fight with each other over the Atlantic ahead of Noah's second European tour. This agreement to no longer fly together happened by common consent, without it ever having to be formalized between them.

'That's good, you guys read. We'll be here if you need anything,' the man beside Noah said to the kids in front. There was no response from the two children, who were both completely engrossed in their literature already. Noah tried to ignore the whole clan and finally get down to his one-way conversation with an Allah he had never believed in. But when the man and woman next to him began conversing with each other, he found it impossible to ignore their dialogue.

'I never flew business class until I was twenty-eight,' the man said. The woman giggled flirtatiously at her co-carer's confession.

'Really? When I was a kid that was the only way we ever flew. My mother would have stood for no less.'

Noah felt a surge of rage stir within him as he thought about his own deprived childhood. He suppressed it and continued casually eavesdropping on the conversation going on beside him.

'So, your parents were wealthy?' the man asked the woman.

'Not as rich as you'd think given their lifestyle. My folks always lived beyond their means. Somehow, it never caught up with them.'

She looked off into the distance with glassy eyes. Noah thought for a moment that she might be drunk but quickly dispelled this hypothesis. It seemed instead as if something she considered profound had occurred to her for the first time.

'I don't know how they managed to pull that off for as long as they did,' she said finally. The man and the woman both laughed nervously at one another. Noah was completely baffled. The couple seemed to be travelling with children who they both had some sort of parental responsibility for, yet here they were talking to one another as if they were on a first date. As their conversation progressed, they said even more things which revealed their utter ignorance of one another. He examined their hands: neither wore rings. Noah listened as if he was going to be quizzed later on the discussion's details as it continued, punctuated with excessive giggling from both parties and accidental touching of each other's extremities. Yet he got no further on as to figuring out what their relationship consisted of and how they ended up in the business class section of a plane going from Los Angeles to New York saddled with joint custody of two children despite hardly knowing one another. At one point, the young girl in front of Noah turned around and faced the woman beside him by kneeling on her seat.

'Joan, I need the bathroom. Do you think you're allowed to use them while the flight is still on the ground?'

'In business class I'm sure it won't be an issue, sweetie.'

As the girl got up to go to use the facilities, Noah found his head swirling. He suddenly felt a bit ill. A dark thought occurred to him as he watched the young girl open the door to the toilet and enter its confines: *I wish I had a bomb on me so that I could blow this plane to smithereens.* The root of his anger was, of course, the fact that none of the clan, not the man nor the woman nor the children they were mysteriously carting around the country, not one of them seemed to recognize him in the slightest. He was happy to be identified correctly and then despised – but to remain anonymous, to anyone, anywhere, was simply unacceptable.

Given all this, Noah did something semi-drastic next. He called for the stewardess, who promptly trotted over.

'Sorry for the delay, sir, but I can assure you we will be in the air shortly.'

'I want to switch seats.'

The air hostess was genuinely stunned by this request and took a moment to gather her wits.

'Is there something wrong with the seat, sir?'

'No, I just want to sit somewhere else. Another part of the plane.'

'The flight is fully booked, I'm afraid, sir.'

Noah thought for a moment about pulling a pop star style full-on diva tantrum, full of 'I'm a goddamn spokesperson for this airline' type of ranting (which he wasn't at the time, but as mentioned before, had been previously). However, he thought better of it. Not for any reason other than the desire to conserve energy. He took a moment to consider his options and then decided on his next move.

'I would be happy to sit in economy if that's all that's available.'

The air hostess laughed out loud, mostly out of sheer surprise. This, needless to say, was not a request she had ever previously come across nor could have ever conceived of being subjected to.

'Are you serious, sir?'

'One hundred per cent.'

Noah got up and brushed past the air hostess. He found himself vaguely aroused until he remembered her boyish ass, which threw water on the fire.

'You come with me to economy,' Noah said to her. 'I'll walk through and look for a seat I like. When I find it, I will offer whoever is sitting there my seat and if they like the sound of the deal, we switch.'

'As long as you're sure about this, sir. I'll remind you now, it's a long flight.'

'Completely sure.'

As soon as Noah opened the curtain and started to walk down the aisle towards the back of the plane, he got what he had subconsciously been after. He was immediately recognized by at least ninety per cent of the passengers, all of whom started to whisper and point at the pop star. The atmosphere became highly charged as more and more of the plane became aware of the fact that they were in the presence of Noah Hastings, a god who had decided on a whim to come down to earth. The only annoyance was Noah catching Jules and his other lackeys out of the corner of his eye, all of them now wondering what they should do in response to this unprecedented event.

'Excuse me, sir, I'm sorry to bother you,' Noah said to a man sat in an aisle seat who had watched Hastings walk towards him as if Noah were Jesus coming back to enact the Rapture. He was in his early twenties, slightly spotty with a pronounced dandruff problem. 'But if you would care to switch seats with me, I'd be most obliged. All you need to do is say "yes" and this lovely lady here' – he pointed to the stewardess – 'will take you to your new seat, which is a perfectly acceptable one located in the business-class portion of the aeroplane.'

The man with the moon eyes looked as if he had a million things to say. In the end all he could manage to get out was:

'Yes.'

Noah offered the man his hand, which was taken with almost surreal affection. He then got up out of his seat, not taking his eyes off of Noah for a single microsecond. His gaze stayed on the pop star who had appeared out of the ether, even as he got his carry-on out from the overhead compartment.

'*Party at My Place* is the greatest fucking album of all time. Needed to say that,' he said as he finally broke off his stare and turned to face where he was now headed, onward towards his extremely lucky break.

Noah sat down in his new, markedly less comfortable seat and started to flip through the glossy magazine he'd bought before boarding. He stopped randomly on a page that had an article about a notably tall woman, 6'5" she was, and her relationship with her husband, who was 5'3".

'I love to dominate a man in bed,' says the giant woman, 'and the

101

only way I can ever get that feeling in the way I need it is if the guy is really short. Also, Ernie is a totally nice guy and that helps a bunch'.

God, western civilization is so fucked up and wrong. Why do people exhibit themselves in such a shameless way, discussing their weird sex lives with a trashy magazine? He then laughed out loud as the realization hit him that he, Noah Hastings, a world-famous pop star who would rather sit in economy class than have to suffer in obscurity for even the duration of a plane ride, was now mentally lecturing people about being exhibitionists.

'You're Noah Hastings, aren't you?' asked the guy beside Noah that he hadn't noticed before that moment. He felt annoyed at having to deal one-on-one with a pleb until he remembered that he had brought this completely upon himself.

'That's me,' Noah said flatly, not even bothering to look in the enquirer's direction.

'I have to admit something to you . . .'

The man paused, licking his lips as if this action would draw his next set of words forward. He then leaned in towards Noah until he got so close that the pop star could smell his neighbour's halitosis.

'I've never much cared for your material.'

He said it in that smug, I-bet-you've-never-heard-this-one-before sort of a way that people whom Noah met who were not fans of his pretty much always phrased these sorts of put downs. This was the man with the smelly breath's extremely rare chance to bring a genuinely famous person back down to size, and he was not the type of guy to let that all too precious opportunity go to waste.

'Well, that makes two of us,' Noah said, his stock answer in such situations. It usually got a laugh from the hater, who deep-down thought that being hostile was a clever way to earn the respect of the famous individual. But this guy thought it particularly amusing. He even literally slapped his knee.

'Good one there, Hastings. Name's Andy.'

Andy held out his hand towards Noah. The pop star thought

about ignoring the gesture completely and then remembered that he wasn't in business class any longer. Moreover, he was firmly amongst the proles and was stuck with them for the next five and a half hours, so he'd best behave himself. Noah gave Andy his right hand without moving his head even slightly.

'You don't need to tell me your name. That must be the weirdest thing about being really famous, now that I think about it. You never need to introduce yourself to people 'cause everyone already knows who you are! Man, that'd be weird.'

'Yeah, it is kind of weird.'

What else was one supposed to say when people pointed this out? Noah had actually spent time, downtime backstage by himself when he couldn't be bothered to read any of the books he'd bought, or to call someone he knew, or even to masturbate, thinking about a snappy, witty comeback to this droll observation that someone made to him at least once a month. But he could never come up with anything, so all he could reply with was an affirmation. *Yes, it is weird when everyone in the world knows your name.* An existential dilemma lost completely, it seems, on people like those bizarre rich pricks he'd abandoned in business class and their modern, who the hell knows what exactly was going on family arrangement, that he found he couldn't spend a whole flight surrounded by, even though it meant giving up his seat in the nice portion of the plane.

Noah then found himself once again trying to puzzle out the couple he'd left behind in business class and what precisely their situation was before shaking his head and resting his thoughts elsewhere with great effort. He managed to think about some of the strange books he'd been reading recently, stuff he'd flipped through when he wasn't spending his backstage downtime trying to come up with pithy responses and failing. He'd recently attempted to read a book written by the feted intellectual Jadran Babic and found he could get past page twenty; it became all about having to look up yet another word online – the final straw was 'rhizomatic' – before throwing the book across the room in disgust. Prior to treating the Babic book in this manner, Noah hadn't thrown a piece of reading material across a room in disgust since his childhood (when he used to do it every other day). He tried to remember the last time he'd done this before the Babic incident but struggled. Until it popped into his head: *Gareth Gates: Right from the Start*. He'd been in his room in the trailer they were living in at the time. It was partly out of jealously, partly out of the poor quality of the book as a piece of literature. He must have been twelve, thirteen at the time.

This throwing of the book to the wall had prompted John K. Smiley, who was staying with the Hastings at the time for reasons that Noah never fully understood – Smiley always seemed to have money and the Hastings always seemed to be broke, yet Smiley was the one who was always preying on the Hastings' hospitality – to enter Noah's room unprompted and uninvited.

'Hey, sport,' Smiley said, his usual vaguely unsettling for reasons you could never fully grasp smile spread across his face. 'I heard a noise and figured I'd check and see if you was all right and all.'

Noah didn't know what to say. Abraham forbade him bringing any books into the house, and the biography of a sinful British pop singer would have done who knows what to Abraham's temper. As a result, it was within Noah's interests to play everything down and try and get rid of Smiley as quickly as possible.

'It was some school books. I couldn't understand my homework and I was frustrated. Anyways, I best get back to it. Thanks for checking on me, Mr Smiley.'

Noah could tell from Smiley's gait that he had no plans to leave the kid's bedroom so prematurely.

'You're so darn bookish, son. You need to mellow out some. Why don't you step outside with me and have a beer?'

It was then that Noah recalled that his parents were out for the evening, who knew where. The idea of a beer with Smiley appealed to him for various reasons. It was a chance to find out more about

Smiley, a man who had been in and around his life for years of whom Noah knew little that was concrete at the time. Also, the situation was watertight: how could Smiley rat on him without implicating himself for feeding him alcohol?

Noah was bumped out of his reverie of the time he and Smiley had had that first beer together, the evening their bizarre relationship officially kicked itself off, by Andy digging his elbow sharply into Noah's ribs.

'So, what do you think?' Andy said as he did so. Noah hadn't noticed that Andy had been speaking the whole time that his thoughts had been elsewhere, stuck in the Smiley infected past.

'Sorry, I wasn't listening,' Noah confessed in a non-apologetic, matter-of-fact tone of voice. This was the wrong thing to say; it was exactly the moment that Andy had been hoping for and thought he would have had to have worked a lot harder to get.

'So, Mr Pop Star can't be bothered to listen to the ramblings of a common citizen then, is that it? I get it, I get it. Hey, I have an idea: why don't I listen to one of your shitty songs and try and forget all about it. Oh wait, all your songs suck, I forgot!'

A young man who was sitting in the one of the middle seats adjacent to Noah laughed raucously at Andy's comment. Several people in the area giggled as well. One older woman actually found it all so amusing she had to put her hand to her mouth to restrain herself. Noah was about to respond when Jules picked the worst possible time to finally come over and check in.

'Hey, boss. Everything all right? Did they kick you out of business class for something?'

This was manna to Andy who started to laugh so hard he turned a shade of purple.

'I'm fine, Jules. Go tell everyone over there to mellow out. I came to sit here by choice.'

Jules was confused, but then again, he worked for a confusing individual so he was used to it.

'Whatever, boss. You know where I am if you need anything.'

With Jules having mercifully withdrawn from the picture, Noah decided he'd had enough of Andy and his taunting.

'Listen, asshole, I've had about enough of the bullshit, do I make myself understood?' Noah asked rhetorically. He was about to grab Andy's collar as an aggressive gesture, but stopped as a stewardess, a much less attractive one than the woman who had brought him here and deposited him in his current lumpenproletarian surroundings, boy's butt or no boy's butt, was standing over both Noah and Andy.

'I will put the both of you off the plane if I hear another peep, is that clear?'

Noah was about to say something, to protest, to give a sort of 'do you know who the fuck I am?' type of speech; until he realized he had forfeited his right to do so by voluntarily relegating himself to the economy section. As the unattractive stewardess walked away, Andy snickered quietly. *I wish I had a bomb on me right now. Simply to shut these laughing fuckers up for good.* Noah then thought about how he despised his fame, but then when he was stripped of even a narrow portion of its protection, he panicked. He was tired of the tours; of Australia, of Madison Square Garden where he would be performing tomorrow evening, but at the same time he couldn't imagine being able to survive without it all. There was no solution. Except to do something radical, outrageous. Within the few seconds that followed, Noah came up with his plan, fully fleshed out. He would blow himself up on stage the following night during his concert at Madison Square Garden.

The idea landed almost completely fully formed in Noah's mind. He didn't stop to laugh at the absurdity of the plan or to consider its moral dimensions; instead, it all seemed abundantly clear from the moment that he conceived of it that this was something he absolutely had to see through. His mind went immediately to the details: he had to get hold of a bomb that would do the trick. Thankfully, he knew exactly who to call. He'd get in touch with Smiley as soon as he was back on terra firma. This plan formulated, Noah instantly felt a calm come over him he hadn't known in what might have been the whole of his pop career. A Zen oneness of the kind that he'd been searching for endlessly; a craving that had ultimately been the thing that had carried him to Mr Elahi and his mosque every day during his 'Muslim period'; that made him put up with an endless stream of people he should have known better than to have wasted time on, like Eva; all of it in the vain search for the feeling he had in abundance at that moment, sitting in economy class for the next five and a half hours, beside some obnoxious asshole who was laughing at him, having chosen to end his life voluntarily within the next thirty-six hours. Noah felt so good, in fact, that he decided to befriend his nemesis for the hell of it.

'Look, Andy, I'm sorry for what I said. I think we got off on the wrong foot. I should never have called you an asshole. Peace?'

This caught Andy off-guard and he stopped his sardonic giggling. This was actually Andy's fantasy version of events playing out in reality, of course – him showing up a world-famous celebrity and said star then finding himself beat, thus supplicating himself to Andy's will and patronage.

'Of course, Noah. I appreciate the apology. And now, I got an idea,' Andy said and then jumped up out of his seat, squeezing past Noah and then reaching up into the overhead compartment (it should be noted that the plane was still on the ground at the time). He emerged from up top with a case of beer. Samuel Johnson, no less.

'I was saving this for tonight but what the hell,' Andy said, partly to himself and partly to Noah. He then extracted two beers from the box and handed one to his newfound famous friend. He then hurriedly extracted a bottle opener from his front pocket, one resting on his keychain, and opened both Noah's and his own beer in quick succession.

'Here's to a beautiful friendship, Noah Hastings.'

'Here's to a beautiful friendship, Andy insert surname here.'

Andy found this genuinely amusing and did a bit of a spit-take on the beer he'd swilled while Noah was mid-toast. The two men proceeded to down the rest of the case during the flight, talking about a variety of topics that Noah would not have thought Andy capable of discussing when first the two met.

'A school shooting in the name of Noah Hastings', Nina Hargreaves, *Washington Telegraph*, November 13th, 2021

Another day, another school shooting in America. This is the twenty-seventh this year; it has come to the point that a student walking into his or her school and gunning down his or her classmates needs an addendum to the story in order to make it newsworthy. As it happens, this mass atrocity in Sacroslitto, California has such a detail.

Nine children dead, two adults slain, eleven injured. Shooter was named Thompson P. Ichabod, described, as is always the case when it comes to school-orientated murderers where the assailant is roughly the same age as his victims, as a quiet loner who was an average student. Today's story is, as ever, simple enough to describe: Ichabod entered Jared Corey Kushner High School at 11:13 a.m. this morning and walked calmly around the school, spraying anyone and everyone who came his way with bullets emitted from his high-powered assault rifle. What makes this stand out from other school shootings, which have tragically become ubiquitous in American life, is what Ichabod's stated motivation for the killings were: to honour his hero, Noah Hastings.

We know this from the plethora of writings Ichabod left behind in his bedroom. Notebooks filled with what could be seen as his 'school shooting manifesto' are outlined with descriptions of what he planned to do (all of which has now come to pass) and why. It has something to do with Hastings as a sort of martyr for the failings of 'the white race', with the pop star seen by Ichabod as the last true man. He puts Noah Hastings at the top of a pantheon of heroes which include Adolf Hitler. He describes the loss of the south in the US Civil War as 'history's greatest tragedy'. In other words, Thompson Ichabod was a white supremacist, one who saw Noah Hastings as a man after his own heart.

This is, in a sense, meaningless: Ichabod was clearly mentally disturbed, and whatever he chose to read into Noah Hastings' life and the musician's motivations for his corresponding act of mass murder is largely irrelevant. Except that it does open up the debate as to how we react to these sorts of incidents – and what we think they mean about the manner of threats we currently face as a nation.

This debate is already being shut down as I write this article. Fox News leads the way, describing the white supremacist angle on the Ichabod school shooting as a 'red herring'.

'I wouldn't be surprised if a lot of the stuff pointing in that particular direction has been planted by the FBI itself,' said Judge Garry Carlson, the right's leading conspiracy theorist these days. 'It's part of a liberal plot to divert attention away from Islam. They want it to be anyone else's fault, so why not land it on the Nazis, right?'

One has to wonder why the FBI, who are clearly desperate to solve this case any which way, would divert attention away from where they are most likely to find the actual conspirators in the Noah Hastings bombing case. Except I'm now going down a Judge Garry-created rabbit hole and better stop while I'm not too far down.

What I feel like at the moment, in amongst a shouting pack of reporters in small-town California, is that we are lost in a web of lies as a nation. One side wishes to use the Noah Hastings bombing to persecute Muslims; the other wishes to use things like the Ichabod school shooting as proof positive that Islam was not in any way involved in the Noah Hastings bombing. Neither camp is right – in fact, both are mostly wrong on almost every imaginable count. Those of us caught in the middle, simply trying to report the truth, are frankly getting sick of it. When are we going to stop politicizing the murder of children in America?

'What Noah Hastings' death meant to me', by Ron O'Nair, an article in *Pink Baby* magazine, November 2021 edition

I am similar in age to Noah Hastings. Or rather I was. For while I go on ageing, he lies in pieces at the back of some FBI laboratory somewhere. Mostly as a result of this rough concurrence at the start of our lives, it was through Noah Hastings that I first discovered my sexuality. I say mostly because the fact that we were close in age was key to the connection.

I knew I was gay before I first laid eyes on Hastings, all buff and tanned and dancing for his life in a cheesy pop video, I being seventeen at the time and he eighteen. But something about seeing that video crystallized in a way that nothing previously in my life had ever done what my sexual identity was – and what that really meant. I'd had plenty of crushes on boys in my classes, men on TV, male teachers. Yet I had never felt such a rush of lust as when I caught that initial glimpse of Noah Hastings' torso.

I never got the same sexual hit again from Hastings as I did on that first viewing, although something about the whole experience acted as an epiphany. I knew I couldn't hide my sexuality any longer – it became completely impossible somehow. I came out to my parents, who – surprise, surprise – were already completely aware of the fact that I'm gay, and had been for the entirety of my life. There are few anti-climaxes in the world like being a ball of nervous energy for days, terrified of telling your father you're a homosexual, before finally blurting it out and having him say, in a very droll way: 'Yeah, no shit, son. Thanks for the memo.'

At that tender an age, even in the fairly upmarket bit of Chicago I lived in during my late teens, it was tough being openly gay. I probably did myself no favours by flaunting it a little after I'd come out, desperate as one can be at that stage of their life to demonstrate that you won't be bullied by anyone. I was bullied, of course, and the scars still run deep. Girls that I had become friends with, confidants, could turn on me so easily when their meathead boyfriends decided to engage in a little homo-bashing. The number of times I came home crying because some girl that I thought I had known so well had cackled evilly while her man pushed me around, shouting that fags have AIDS and should be killed, was sadly more than I can reliably count.

But Noah was always there, dancing away with that exposed torso of his. It always gave me comfort, his music, his promotional material. Until shortly after I turned nineteen, discovered a friend's Depeche Mode songs, and then Noah was all but cast aside.

I hadn't thought about Noah Hastings much in a long time before June 16th brought him into my life front and centre once again. With that came the ugliness of the investigation into why he blew himself up at Madison Square Garden, and its never-ending dead ends. The vacuum of real closure on the Hastings bombing is being filled with lurid conjecture from non-reputable sources instead. We have at the moment the tabloids all crowing about a John K. Smiley character from Noah's past who is apparently the accomplice the FBI has been looking for all this time. How the Islam thing comes into that I have no idea, but I guess you'll have to ask the tabloids. I wouldn't think about it too deeply, however – next week there will be some other flash in the pan who may or may not even exist in reality who was behind it all. Perhaps Jimmy Hoffa is ultimately responsible.

Back to being seventeen: it really sticks with you and as a result the man who sang 'You're in My Heart Forever' never entirely escaped from my own. I remained thankful to him for lighting the spark that led to the whole rest of my life. Because while it was a pain in the ass to be bullied in Bucktown, truth was I wouldn't have made the friends that I made either, friends I still have and cherish, even now that I live in the Big Apple. Had I not made those friends I probably would have made different choices, choices that would have led me down a different path. Which means I wouldn't be doing what I do now, which is what I love more than anything, nor would I be with my wonderful boyfriend of four years, Mike. I don't know where I'd be, and perhaps I'd be somewhere equally wonderful, but I can't know that for sure, and part of me feels like I almost certainly wouldn't trade the not-discovering-Noah Hastings-at-seventeen life for the one I actually have.

However, I put 'remained' as opposed to the present tense of the word for a reason. Because after the events of June 16th, 2021, I feel I have to close that seventeen-year-old part of me off, this time for ever. When your saviour turns out to be a suicidal murderer who was motivated by a creed that wishes to execute people like me, then I'm afraid the deal between myself and Noah Hastings must come to an end. I wish it wasn't so. Yet he was the one who went and blew himself up, so it's not my fault.

I can't go on holding a flame for a mass murderer, however great a part he played in helping me to form my identity. There has to be a line in the sand, and someone who ideologically takes the lives of ninety-one innocent people is certainly way over mine. I wish I could say we'll always have 'You're in My Heart Forever' but we won't. Because Noah Hastings, after the events of last summer, is no longer in my heart. Instead there is a Noah-sized hole that will remain as a reminder, for as long as I live, of what happened at Madison Square Garden one horrible evening.

'Was THIS man responsible for the Noah Hastings bombing?', an article in the *National Requester*, November 30th, 2021 by Margaret Bagnall

It looks as if the whole idea of the Noah Hastings bombing being linked to Islamic terrorism is a complete sham, the *National Requester* is proud to report. As an explosive article in the *Washington Telegraph* revealed last month, the FBI is in meltdown mode after several high-level leaks about how badly the investigation is now going hit the news. It has now been revealed, in a *National Requester* exclusive, that Amir Elahi, the FBI's one arrest in regard to the Noah Hastings investigation, HAS BEEN RELEASED WITHOUT CHARGE. That's right: having held Amir Elahi in custody for several weeks, the FBI have been forced to let the Los Angeles-based Islamic preacher go free. This is because, as sources close to the *National Requester* both inside and outside the FBI have told us, the main suspect in the whole case now appears to be a Christian preacher named John K. Smiley, a friend of Noah's late father, Abraham Hastings. As not many people are aware, Noah's father had a history of criminal scams that put him behind bars not once but twice, and the Robin to his Batman (if Batman and Robin were bad guys) was none other than Smiley, a fellow preacher and con man getting as much as he could from his turf in the deep south of this land.

What is there to say about John K. Smiley? Plenty – at least in this *National Requester* scoop there is. Smiley and Abraham Hastings met in prison when they were both in their twenties. It was friendship at first scam: the two bonded over a gambling con they both had going simultaneously.

'Those two were inseparable,' said Tony 'Baloney' Grabawski, an inmate of the Louisiana State Penitentiary at the same time both Abraham Hastings and John K. Smiley were interred. 'They talked a lot about all the stuff they were going to do once they were on the outside again. Most of it was scams but they were also dead serious about the whole onward Christians soldiers stuff.'

Another former inmate told us, in an exclusive interview with *National Requester*, all about the way of thinking that these two young, budding criminals used to motivate each other.

'They talked a lot about how scamming the church was okay because the church wasn't doing the things it was supposed to be doing. You know, it wasn't gaining ground on atheism and Islam and whatever else, it was plain losing it. And Hastings and Smiley, they figured, well, the only way to gain that ground back again was to rip off the mainstream church and use the money to create a sort of Christian Al-Qaeda kind of thing.'

Coming soon to the *National Requester* and the *National Requester* only: an exclusive interview with John K. Smiley. We think we've almost found him – but he is harder to track down than an available taxi in Los Angeles. However, we will not fail you, *National Requester* readers. Keep reading.

A Nina Hargreaves comment piece entitled 'Salima Malik, Louisiana, and Islamophobia in America', *Washington Telegraph*, December 4th, 2021

Salima Malik, mother of two boys, was walking her children to school Tuesday morning of last week. As she drew close to her sons' school she was approached by a group of young men. They taunted her about her appearance – she was wearing a head scarf and a salwar kameez – calling her 'Muslamic scum'. Salima attempted to ignore the abuse and walk on, but one of her children decided to call the men out on their idiotic racism. At this point, the four young men, all aged between fifteen and seventeen, physically assaulted Salima Malik. In broad daylight, on the streets of New York City, she was punched and kicked, in front of her two sons, Adil and Thomas, who are six and eight years old respectively, as they were held back by their arms and forced to watch. She was hurt badly enough to sustain injuries requiring medical attention. Her assailants told her during this malicious but mercifully brief assault that, and I quote, 'America doesn't need your kind anymore'.

I wish I could say that the Salima Malik incident was an isolated one. Yet a similar thing happens somewhere in America almost every day. A random attack by strangers on an innocent victim, all because they happen to carry outward signs of being Muslim. The only reason the attack on Salima was truly notable was that it occurred in Manhattan, a location most people assume would be immune to such types of behaviour.

What makes this trend all the worse is that the FBI's summer announcement about the links between the Hastings' bombing and

116

radical Islam is beginning to look increasingly premature. Six weeks ago, the Bureau made its first arrest in the entire investigation. Amir Elahi, an LA-based imam who had known Noah Hastings and had by his own admission spent time with the pop star on the day of the incident, was released without charge, after being detained briefly for questioning. This apparently leaves the Hastings bombing case back at square one. Sources within the FBI have themselves stated that the investigation has been a terrible one, as I uncovered in an article for the *Telegraph* at the end of October.

Given where the FBI's search for the facts surrounding the Noah Hastings bombing appears to be aimed at present, with its one arrest now come to nothing, we should all begin to seriously question the basis of the investigation itself. In other words, it is time ask ourselves whether we can go on believing that Islamic fundamentalism was the underlying inspiration for the Noah Hastings bombing. We as a nation owe it to people like Salima Malik to find out for certain.

In questioning what the ideological reason for the Noah Hastings incident was, we should start with the facts as we have them. We know for certain that Hastings had a secret Islamic past; that he'd spent time attending a mosque near his home in Los Angeles. There seems to be reliable enough evidence that he went there almost every day during an eleven-week stretch roughly three years prior to the MSG bombing. Amir Elahi has said as much and other witnesses support this version of events. We also know that Amir Elahi flew to New York to visit Noah Hastings on June 16th, the day the bombing occurred, and returned to Los Angeles that same day. There were also several books with an Islamic theme (including the Koran itself) among Hastings' belongings in his dressing room.

This is the sum total of all there is in the public domain as supposed proof that the Islamic fundamentalism theory is the correct one. Sources within the FBI itself have also told me recently that there is nothing else in terms of hard evidence not in the public realm to support the hypothesis.

Which brings us to John K. Smiley. For weeks now, many tabloid newspapers in America have been running a story about a man with this name; a Baptist minister from Hastings' childhood who it has been alleged via far from solid journalistic sources (this is putting it mildly) may have been directly involved in the Hastings bombing. As such, the Smiley lead has been dismissed as a non-story, and Smiley himself a tabloid creation. I thought it was worth finding out for certain whether or not the Smiley story had any genuine merit. I wanted to find out first whether the man himself even exists, in itself not a certainty. Thus, I did what strangely no other journalist in the country had done already: I jumped on a plane to Louisiana and did some digging around.

The town Noah Hastings spent more time living in as a child than any other, Fausse Route (which is French for 'wrong way'), is predictably depressing and nondescript. The people were stereotypically open and inviting however, and this immediately paid dividends. I dug up this quote on my first day in town, looking through old, local press clippings:

'The problem we got at the moment is that these Muslims are training their kids to do anything for the cause. Give their lives in felling the enemy as a for instance . . . it don't get more committed than that, does it? That's why we lost in Vietnam – we had the superior armoury, but Charlie had the will. We had a bunch of stoned idiots, wandering around in a haze, smoking dope and listening to Jimi Hendrix, while they had kids strapping bombs to themselves and diving under tanks. Now, if we could get our kids to that point, where they were willing to strap bombs to themselves, wander into the Iranian palace and blow up the Shah, man, then we'd really have a chance against Islam.'

That's attributed to Abraham Hastings, quoted in the local *Fausse Route Tribune* shortly after his son's initial brush with fame. It's a quote that made me physically unwell when I first read it; the part about kids strapping bombs to themselves summoning forth the visceral horror of the June 16th bombing itself. Once I had gotten over myself, I then wondered why no national outlet had picked it up when it was first printed. Even more bizarre is the fact that I'm the first journalist on a national newspaper since the Hastings bombing to spot the quote and reprint it.

Abraham Hastings and his strange life has received incredibly little attention given the surreal shadow it throws over his son's murder/suicide. He was a Baptist preacher, this much is certain; he was also a small-time crook. He moved his family around the south during Noah's childhood, usually to evade arrest. Fausse Route was the one town he kept coming back to, for reasons unknown. Even when Abraham was caught by police, the trial would almost always come to nothing, as his flock refused to bear witness against him, despite having been swindled by the man. However, he did do two short stints in the Louisiana state penitentiary. On the first of these, undertaken when he was a young man and Noah Hastings was still in his mother's womb, he met a man who was to be a lifelong friend – in Abraham Hastings' universe, a rare thing. His name was Jeremiah Samson, but he tended to go by a revolving set of aliases, even within his personal life.

The two men became partners, in terms of both running small-time scams and in producing propaganda of the kind the quote in the *Fausse Route Tribune* will have no doubt acted as a taster. The two published several pamphlets, none of them extant in any form, sadly, around the topic of what can only be described as Christian fundamentalist terrorism.

I visited each of the eleven Christian organizations that Abraham Hastings was known to have worked for or with in Louisiana alone. At one location around fifty miles outside of Fausse Route, I was provided with this quote from Reverend William Gene, someone who worked with Noah Hastings for awhile (he says it was for 'around four or five months'):

'Oh yeah, Hastings, he was a real crook, he was. I knew it from the moment I laid eyes on him. Some of our parishioners took rather longer to reach the same conclusion, if you catch my drift here. Anyway, yeah, I remember a guy named Smiley all right. Can't recall the first name, but Smiley, man, that's not a last name anyone is about to forget in a hurry, now are they? He was a real crook too. Gave me the willies even more than Hastings did. At least Hastings had that kid with the voice – man, that kid could sing up a storm! Smiley hung around in the background most of the time. At least it seemed to me anyways. A real shadowy figure. Whether he was involved in the scam that made Hastings run from these parts, I don't know. He didn't strike me as the type of character to hang around the scene of the crime, if you know what I mean.'

Bringing this all back to Salima Malik and her two boys, Adil and Thomas: regardless of what the truth about Noah Hastings' motivation for what he did on June 16th and whatever the ideology of those who were involved in that crime may have been, what happened to Salima and her family last week was wrong. Yet if it turns out that we have been incorrect this whole time about what happened on June 16th – that Islam was in no way connected to the bombing at Madison Square Garden on that night – the wrongs done to Salima Malik and every other Muslim in this country since the FBI told us about the supposed connect between the two things becomes even more horrific. My brief trip to Louisiana last week made me think that could be possible. Although in the interest of full disclosure I must say that John K. Smiley remains as ephemeral to me as he has done to the Federal Bureau of Investigation and every other journalist in America. Nonetheless, Salima Malik and every other American Muslim should be considered innocent until proven guilty.

'What Nina Hargreaves being fired means to free speech in this country' by Mohammed Qasim, guest commentary piece in the *New York Express*, December 11th, 2021

I must admit to something before we begin. Nina Hargreaves is a dear friend of mine, someone I have known for a great many years. Having said that, even if I did not know her personally, I would still feel aggrieved for what she has been made to suffer this past week.

On December 4th, Nina became the first journalist at a reputable daily newspaper to report on the figure known (possibly apocryphally) as John K. Smiley and his alleged connection to the Noah Hastings bombing. In doing so she appears to have broken an unwritten rule of conduct in early-20s America: she doubted the authenticity of the connection between radical Islamism and the bombing of June 16th. For this supposed crime, she was fired yesterday evening. The official story released by the *Telegraph* is that Nina had broken the terms of her contract by 'misappropriating organizational resources'. The nexus of this explanation is that Nina crossed a line in using her expenses to fund a trip to Louisiana to investigate the Smiley story at source. While her contract states that she can use her expenses to travel when necessary, they can only be used in connection with a Washington-based, political story. Given they felt the trip to Louisiana contravened this, they have said that they felt they had no choice but to let her go.

This is obviously a smokescreen. It has been apparent that the *Telegraph* has wanted to be rid of Nina since late October, when she first exposed the incompetence of the FBI investigation of the

Hastings bombing, via internal Bureau sources. The Louisiana expenses excuse was simply a convenient legal way of executing something they had wanted to do for several weeks. One of their most esteemed journalists had decided they wanted to look into the facts of the Hastings bombing instead of drinking the Kool-Aid as everyone else had done to that point. She has paid a high price for doing so.

My chief worries about Nina Hargreaves being fired by the *Washington Telegraph*, beyond those pertaining to a good friend and her welfare, are around the future of free speech in America. Whatever the truth of the matter – although we should all at least agree that the Hastings incident being Islamically motivated should be placed in some extreme doubt at this stage – Nina simply looked into another possible theory of how events unfolded on June 16th. This is what journalists should be doing. It is their job. We want our best reporters to be continually questioning the official version of events. Although she did not confirm the identity of John K. Smiley nor the connection of anyone bearing that name to the Hastings bombing, she did uncover some interesting information about Abraham Hastings and his advocating of a version of Christianity which can only be described as fundamentalist/terrorist. This information should be followed up on. It will not be by Nina, unfortunately, that much is certain. Any others who may be tempted by how far she managed to get with the story on minimal resources will be warned off by the action the *Telegraph* has taken towards her this week. If it can lead to the firing of Nina Hargreaves, one of the most respected investigative journalists in America, no one can consider themselves immune from personal harm in pursuing this particular story.

I have begun to believe that there is an official cover-up taking place about what happened on June 16th of this year. The FBI were quick to lay the blame at the feet of Islamic fundamentalism, a link that has not been proven in any way whatsoever in the ensuing six months. The media should be looking to expose the reasons behind this, not punishing their own kind when they attempt to do so. In terminating the contract of Nina Hargreaves, the *Telegraph* have done every journalist in America a great disservice. They have also done a disservice to the truth, which is much worse.

June 16th, part four (Trying to find the Koran)

After staring at the Lennon monument for five minutes, recalling the booze-fuelled plane ride of the previous day in excruciating detail, a small East Asian boy pops Noah's bubble by tapping lightly on the pop star's knee repeatedly with a small toy. It's a robotic-looking thing, the toy, something suitably of the culture of which the boy is a part. Noah is about to say something when the boy's father starts to shout at him in Japanese. With that, the child possessing the robot toy stops bothering the pop star and runs off, his father then having to chase him while shouting in his native tongue the whole way.

His attention now back on more immediate concerns, Noah decides to head back to the hotel and make damn sure he knows exactly how to work the bomb Smiley had left for him. As soon as he had arrived at JFK the previous day, Noah found himself a quiet corner and phoned John. Strangely, Smiley seemed like he'd been expecting the call, even though that was impossible. John asked for Noah's hotel room number, which the pop singer was always given in advance, ironically enough, for security reasons. The crooked preacher said the bomb would be waiting at the bottom of the closet for Noah, in a silver flight kit, underneath all of the bed linen. When he had arrived in his room the previous night, the first thing Noah did was check that the silver case was indeed there, throwing aside blankets to do so, even though he knew beyond any shadow of a doubt that it would be there. Noah had then stared at the flight kit for a few seconds but took his investigation no further. Smiley could well have delivered unto him an empty flight case; Noah knew he wouldn't have. There was definitely a bomb in there. He wasn't ready to face it, drunk as hell, at whatever ungodly hour it was, just as he wasn't ready to face it the next morning either.

Is Noah ready to look at the bomb post-Lennon monument, Central Park outing replete with Hare Krishna moment and bizarre Smiley rendezvous? Answer: not yet. Once back in his hotel room, having walked back the exact way he had come only this time without any incident whatsoever, he turns on the TV, which will be the precursor to one thing: more hotel porn. Noah detests all other forms of televisual entertainment including movies. He hadn't even sat through his own piece of cinematic bilge, the stupid monkey movie, though that was hardly a stringent example of his aversion. Noah flips around the 'porn guide' on channel 34, not finding anything that jumps out at him, other than *Office Sluts,* which he'd beaten off to already. In the end, he settles on simply giving *Office Sluts* another twirl through sheer lack of a better idea. He is almost there, as these things go, when there comes a knock at the door. *It's the cleaning staff being overzealous. Didn't give them enough time to change the room while I was out.* He thinks for a moment about whether he had hung the appropriate warning on his outer doorknob and then remembers that he definitely had (having performed this exercise as a way of putting off peering at the bomb further, which is the reason that Noah recalls doing it so clearly). *The sign says 'DO NOT DISTURB', lady.* He ignores the knocking further, until the neglected door hammering is followed up by another rapping on Noah's hotel door by knuckles, this time more incessant than ever. He thinks about whether or not it could be one of his security staff, but they'd have called first. Must be the hotel manager come around to 'be nice' and introduce himself. Never normally happened in big cities, just in shitty Midwestern towns, but this had all the hallmarks of such an intervention.

Noah gets up, shuts off the porn, pulls his trousers back up and answers the door. What he sees there is so unexpected he gives off a slight yelp.

'Sorry, Mr Hastings. This was the appointed time, was it not?'

A large chunk of the previous evening that had been missing from his memory up until that moment springs into his consciousness with alarming force. *Fuck. Elahi is here because I called and asked him to come last night when I was hammered.* Noah tries to recall everything that was said, but the exact details are hazy. He remembers begging the imam to come to New York, saying he would pay for the journey. He recalls booking the ticket himself using his laptop. And now here he is: Mr Elahi, a man Noah had thought he'd never again see, standing right in front of him in the doorway to his New York hotel room on his final day on Earth.

'Of course, Mr Elahi, come in, come in.'

The imam enters the room and has a look around. *Trying to find the Koran.* Noah is correct with this thought. Not seeing the holy book laid out anywhere obvious, Elahi looks a touch disappointed.

'What did you want to see me about so urgently, Mr Hastings?'

Noah has nothing to say to the man in front of him. He tries to bring back more of the conversation from last night but can only recall the mundane parts of it he already had done, like arranging the flight. Panic starts to mount in Noah's mind as more and more details of the previous day and night begin to come back to him: on the plane, he and Andy talking about the merits of feminism (or rather, the lack thereof in their collective opinion) while knocking back a healthy amount of Samuel Johnson. Noah recalls that through his drunken haze he was amazed at the time that none of the airline staff had tried to stop them when they took things a step too far and began running around the airplane's interior in various stages of undress; perhaps it was some last vestige of his pop stardom and its ability to circumvent convention asserting itself. The funny thing is that Noah remembers calling Smiley, clear as day, seemingly sober as a judge, and yet the telephonic reach out to Elahi he is still struggling to reshape. *Did I tell Elahi about my plans for this evening?*

'Why don't you come and sit with me on the bed?' Noah finally comes up with, taking a seat himself on the hotel bed and patting the area directly to his left in an unintentionally creepy manner. He instantly realizes that this invitation has come across with more than a slight air of unintended homoeroticism, and the horrified look on Elahi's face that results is the final straw for Noah. The pop star begins to burst into loud, uncontrollable laughter, which emerges from his chest in bursts, almost like sobs. He tries to get a hold of himself, but the more he attempts to do so the more he laughs, until he actually becomes scared he is going to laugh himself to death; die here and now in the hotel room in front of the poor imam who had flown across the entire country to be here, on Noah's request for reasons he can no longer fathom. *Would still be a good story, I guess: pop star laughs himself to death in front of Islamic preacher. The press might think it's some sort of Muslim conspiracy to subvert the minds of western youth.*

During this whole episode, Elahi stands and stares at his ex-pupil, wondering what to do next. Had this happened in Los Angeles, Elahi would have walked out by now, but given he had travelled a long way for no other reason than this meeting, he is inclined to try and give it a greater chance than that.

'Excuse me, Mr Hastings, but what precisely is so humorous?'

Back when Noah would come to the Imam's mosque every day, the spell when he was considering becoming a Muslim (at least as much as he ever would), the way Elahi would say the word 'humorous' would always crack Noah up (something about the accent). The imam using it in this instance was the worst possible thing he could have done. Had he kept quiet, Noah would have calmed down in another thirty seconds, enough to apologize, explain and then at least try and start to have the conversation about why Noah had asked him to come to New York the previous evening. Now Noah is off again, laughing as hard as he ever has in his entire life.

Finally, Noah calms himself down. Yet as he does so, another emotion comes to the surface: anger. Suddenly, he feels unbelievably furious at Amir Elahi, for absolutely no reason. Noah now wants desperately to be rid of the imam but knows that given the man has flown from LA only to see him, there are few ways to get out of this without some form of conversation. Yet he feels unable to speak to Mr Elahi rationally, so he settles for the only possible route, or at least the easiest: he begins to shout at the imam. Loud and as obnoxiously as possible, Noah begins to scream insults at Mr Elahi about his religion, his weakness in coming to New York after they hadn't spoken in three years, his choice of apparel. He even puts in a rant against Pakistani food.

Through all of this, Mr Elahi stands and listens, horrified. Once Noah is through with his rant, he begins hysterically laughing once again. This is the imam's breaking point; he leaves without another word, shutting the door behind him.

It only takes another few seconds for Noah to stop laughing once the imam has departed, but the whole situation seems to cease being so funny almost immediately after the holy man's departure. Shame and guilt settle in, quickly. More and more of the phone conversation he and Elahi had had suddenly reappears in his memory, seconds too late.

'Imam, my man, you must come to New York. You must, at once. This is my hour of need. I require your words, not on the phone, but to my face. Only your God can save me now.'

He said marginally different versions of the same thing, over and over again, until Elahi accepted Noah's offer to pay for a ticket to New York to see him, using the Elahi's evangelical streak and Noah's own fame to manipulate him.

'I have a concert tomorrow night at Madison Square Garden. Twenty thousand young, impressionable minds. I want to convert to Islam myself and then tell these people, these children, that Islam is the way to salvation. But I must have your guidance. I must have you here with me.'

The unconscious reason Noah made the call to Elahi is because he thought that when the imam showed up in New York, if indeed he did, Noah would then be forced to tell him why he had called him there – at which point he would be forced to confess what he was planning on doing at Madison Square Garden with the bomb that was in the closet. With Elahi now gone, Noah's one barrier to committing the act he'd thought up in a drunken moment on an airplane yesterday has been removed. Noah takes a moment to consider how he feels about that. Pretty good, he decides. This pleasant feeling is short lived, however, as it is at this precise moment that the rather unfortunate 'Bob the salesman' incident from the previous evening suddenly reappears in Noah's mind in full Technicolor.

Noah was drinking Jack Daniels and Diet Cokes all by himself in the hotel bar. Jules had tried to talk him into at least drinking in the privacy of his room but Noah was having none of it. He eventually got Jules to leave him alone.

'Is this seat taken?' said a short, bald man who hovered into Noah's view when he was on his seventh JD and fake cola of the evening.

'It is by you now, partner!'

'Thanks. Say, are you that singer guy from the TV?'

'I am that singer guy from the TV.'

'Got a daughter in Delaware. From a previous marriage. Don't see her all that much, but when I talk to her she tells me a lot about your music. Man, she sure is a big fan.'

'How old is she?'

'My daughter? Seven.'

'Jesus, man. Have you heard any of my records? It's not music for seven year olds.'

Bob found this comment mildly amusing.

'I can't make out any of the lyrics and neither can she. Sorry, I can't remember your name, son.'

'It's Noah Hastings.'

'Right, got there, right before you said it. I knew it was biblical. I was about to call you Moses. Name's Bob, by the way.'

'Good to meet you, Bob. And it won't matter what I'm called this time tomorrow.'

'I see. And why won't your name matter this time tomorrow then, as I'm sure you're itching for me to ask?'

'Tomorrow night, Madison Square Garden, I'm going on stage with a big old bomb strapped to my chest. Then I'm going to detonate it, killing myself and whoever's in my path.'

'Right. Where is this bomb right now then? You have to go and pick it up somewhere or do bomb sellers deliver these days?'

Bob the salesman took Noah for drunk; off on some diva-like tangent.

'It's upstairs in my hotel room, right now. You want to come and see it?'

'Now, son, if I didn't know any better I would think you was trying to seduce me.'

'You don't believe me that there's a bomb upstairs in my closet?'

'I think something might be in the closet here, son. Anyways, for the sake of argument, how the hell did you get your bomb into a fancy-ass hotel like this one anyhow?'

'I'm a famous pop star, Bob. As a result, anything is achievable. But in this case, I had a real bona fide terrorist sneak it into my room, all before I arrived.'

'Know a lot of terrorists, do you?'

'Only one. But one's all you need.'

'How did you know which room was going to be yours?'

'The hotel tells you ahead of time. For security reasons.'

This last piece of information Bob took as genuine as well as interesting.

'I did not know that. So, this terrorist, he snuck this bomb into your room then?'

'Yep. Don't know how he did it but I don't need to know, do I?'

'And what is the name of this guy, just in case I should ever need a terrorist to sneak a bomb into a hotel room for me?'

'Calls himself John K. Smiley, but his real handle is Samson. Known him since I was a kid. He was friends with my old man; the two of them used to run scams together.'

'Your old man was a con man?'

'A Baptist preacher, so pretty much, yeah.'

Bob laughed at this line.

'So I can plan ahead a little: you thinking of blowing up this place while you're at it?'

'Don't worry, I'll give you clear notice to skedaddle, friend. What's your room number? I'll slip a note under your door, give you a half hour's notice.'

'Man, you think I'm staying at this ooh-la-la joint? I'm staying at the Ramada down the road. I come in here because the drinks are nicer and I may even make a sale or two.'

'What do you sell, Bob?'

'Aluminium siding.'

'For houses or for any kind of building?'

'If it's upright, we can slather it in aluminium.'

'I like you, Bob. But I'm afraid I'm not interested in buying any aluminium siding right at this juncture.'

'I like you too, Noah. And I sort of figured that out already, but thanks for making it clear.'

Bob the salesman will be traumatized by this conversation for the rest of his days. In the first few weeks following the bombing, Bob thinks endlessly about going to the authorities and telling them about the conversation he'd had with Noah Hastings in the hotel the evening before the bombing. He always stopped himself, having become terrified of being implicated in the whole thing and as a result, he keeps his mouth shut. He, more than most Americans, feels a huge sense of relief when the case is 'solved'.

Panic fills Noah's chest as he recalls these portions of the bar conversation had with Bob the next day, the memory of it all striking him soon after Mr Elahi's departure from the hotel room. He went on to inform the travelling salesman about a load of intricate details, such as the way the bomb had been procured and his hotel room number. Stuff about Smiley's identity was discussed. Taking a deep breath, Noah realizes that there is nothing to be overly concerned about regarding the Bob the salesman incident. First off, the whole thing is completely unbelievable. A world-famous pop star, when shitfaced, tells you he's going to blow himself up on stage the following night. Who would take this at face value? And even if Bob the travelling salesman did think Noah was going to do what he had described, who the hell would listen to him or take his story seriously? Bob probably didn't even think it was actually Noah Hastings he had spoken to, just some joker pretending to be. The fact that the cops hadn't busted down his door that morning spoke to the fact that one or more of these realities had to be true.

Out of the blue, Noah has an epiphany. He realizes why he had unloaded all of that detail on poor, unsuspecting Bob. It was so that Bob would be witness to some crucial information about the whole crime he was intending to perpetrate. Witness to enough clues to nail Smiley big time. Noah smiles at his own subconscious genius. It is actually the sole way that Noah could have passed that information on without damaging the operation itself. Noah knows that Smiley has to go down for his part in what will be one of the crimes of the century. The more he thinks about it, the more he becomes convinced that destroying Smiley's life in the most elaborate way possible has been at least one of the deep down, prime motivations for the bombing all along. This revelation not only doesn't change his mind about going through with the suicide bombing, it in fact strengthens his determination to see it through to the end.

Following the Elahi hotel room visit and the subsequent shock of recalling in full the details of the discussion with Bob the salesman, Noah falls asleep. During this nap, he has a series of predictable dreams, all of them involving being on stage at Madison Square Garden and trying to make a bomb strapped to his person go off and failing to make it happen. They involve Noah mostly pressing the button to activate, like Smiley had shown him all those times, over and over again to no effect. He is in the midst of one of these tedious dreams when he is awoken by someone shaking him. In the dream, this plays out as the hand of God coming down from the sky to stop him from continuing to try and kill himself. Noah looks up, half asleep still, and sees the face of Jules uncomfortably close to his own.

'What the fuck, Jules?'

'KACL interview in forty minutes. I tried calling your cell like, a million times.'

Noah had completely forgotten about this media commitment. He often did forget all about them. He never likes doing interviews, but on this occasion, he feels existentially against participating in one.

'Cancel, Jules. I don't feel well.'

'No can do, boss. This one is a Murray special.'

Jules is referring to things on the agenda that Murray has specifically pointed to as a 'must do'. Usually it has something to do with Noah's manager owing someone a favour of some description. Noah knows that if he bails on a Murray special, he is then likely to be followed around incessantly by his manager, being yelled at for the remainder of the day up until show time. It isn't the berating Noah wants to avoid in particular; rather, given his plans for the evening, the shadowing element could prove counterproductive.

'All right, I'm getting dressed. I'll see you out front in ten.'

Jules would rather it was in five but accepts this is as being as good as it's going to get and leaves his employer in peace to gather himself. Once his personal assistant has left the room, Noah recalls his decision to take the Bible currently resting in the side table's drawer along with him to the venue. He doesn't know if he'll have a chance to come back to the room, so he decides to take it with him to the radio station. He opens the drawer, picks it up, and then places the holy book in his left outside jacket pocket – the copy of *Mein Kampf* he had got from Eva all those years ago already sitting in the right pocket of the garment – as he takes one last look at the hotel room. Noah removes the card key from the wall socket, thus leaving the room in darkness, and departs. As soon as he's in the hotel hallway right outside of his room, it strikes him that he has yet to take even a cursory look at the bomb lying in the bottom of his closet, in the silver flight case, courtesy of John K. Smiley – though it still hasn't occurred to him that he will have to personally return to the room to gather the case in order to get it to the Garden. Noah is too used to things like that being done for him. Instead, he chastises himself as he walks towards the elevator for having not had the courage to have at least taken a maiden peek at the device.

Noah can't recall which station KACL is until they arrive at the studio, at which point several bad memories of the place come flooding forth. That time he'd been called out by the asshole DJ on air for supposedly ripping off the Hollies. The time he had got a blowjob in the toilet from the ugliest woman he'd ever seen up until that point in his life (she would be superseded subsequently, with another woman Noah would have brief and tawdry sexual relations with in another radio station toilet in Sioux Falls, South Dakota). The time Murray gave him a hard time about something or other immediately before the interview, the usual Murray shit about something letting him down that Noah didn't want to hear about, an incident which put Noah in a bad mood before going on air and subsequently led to a flat interview.

'Where's Murray?' Noah asks Jules as they sit in the modest radio station green room, an eighteen-year-old girl with a nose ring off to fetch him a coffee, white, two sugars. Jules shrugs his shoulders. Noah is secretly relieved that his manager isn't present as he is as keen as ever to avoid him on this day of all days.

'Said he'll see us at the Garden,' Jules tells his boss.

'What a prick. Gets me dragged here to do this thing and can't even bother to be here himself.'

The main reason Noah wants to avoid seeing Murray is due to fear of his manager's ability to read his thoughts whenever the two of them are in close physical proximity with each other. Perhaps Murray would figure it out with no verbal clues at all, the way he could figure out everything about Noah bar his penchant for hotel TV porn, which perhaps the manager knows about as well and had kept to himself, waiting for the right time to weaponize it against his client.

'We're ready for you now, Mr Hastings,' says a fresh-faced intern, probably new off the bus from some ghastly Midwestern hamlet. Noah pulls himself to his feet, simply wanting to get the interview over with and out of the way. He cheers up immensely, however, when it occurs to him that this is the last ever radio station bullshit promo interview he will ever have to go through with for the rest of eternity.

'Hello and welcome to KACL, home of New York's best commercial pop and R&B. With us in the studio this afternoon, ahead of his appearance at Madison Square Garden, is the fabulous, the marvellous, the outstanding Noah Hastings. Noah, welcome to the show.'

'It's great to be here, Ned.'

'That's Ted, Ted Power, but you can call me whatever you like Noah, baby.'

Noah switches into autopilot, coughing up the usual crap about how great it is to be in front of the fans every night; how his latest song is the greatest thing he's ever put out; how he'd like to thank the Lord almighty for letting him do what it is he loves doing the most of all. He thinks again about Smiley in the midst of his robotic patter. Noah feels a weird ping of joy that he's going to see the corrupt old prick one more time, of that he feels surer than ever. It was why he hadn't investigated the bomb yet; Smiley would help when the time was right.

That was the thing about Smiley: he'd always been good to Noah.

Kind would be stretching it, since it was always clear that Smiley had some sort of agenda, one that Noah could never fathom but seemed obvious enough to him existed. Smiley always had time for him; he was, thinking back on it, the one adult in his life growing up who had never even attempted to directly abuse him in any way. He helped Noah out in terms of recording his first demos; helped Noah find his feet when he moved to Los Angeles to make it. When he heard Noah was moving to LA, he decided to move there as well, and so the nascent pop sensation stayed a few months at Smiley's new abode, something without which Noah would have struggled to have stayed in the city for the crucial nine months it took to gain a recording contract. Yet Noah had never had anything but hatred in his heart for Smiley, and he had never really understood why. He was always friendly to Smiley's face (why not? When someone's always helping you out, why unnecessarily burn them?), and yet from the moment he had met the man, he had well and truly hated him. Not disliked; it was a pure, unadulterated hatred of the preacher-cum-con man Noah felt.

Noah had spent a great deal of time throughout his adult life agonizing over why this was so. Was it because he couldn't help but hate anyone who was nice to him? He had to admit there was something in that, but it didn't feel like the whole story. Was it that Smiley had led his father astray, getting Abraham involved in a bunch of ploys that sent the old man to prison and then an early grave? This didn't ring true, mostly because Noah had hated his father almost as much as he hated Smiley.

Take the interlude which had cemented Smiley and Noah's 'friendship', when John K. invited a teenaged Noah to share a beer with him after he'd heard him throw the Gareth Gates book against the wall adjacent to the room Smiley had been sitting in at the time.

'Here you go, son,' Smiley had said, handing Noah a can of Miller on the implicit understanding that he drink it. Smiley then cracked one for himself.

'I tell my flock not to partake in liquor. But I myself like to dabble on occasion.'

As Noah half-listens to Ted Power ramble on about some promotion that KACL has on at the moment, all while thinking again about that first beer with Smiley, it suddenly occurs to Noah what it is about Smiley more than anything else that he finds so grating: the man's hypocrisy. This had never previously occurred to Noah. He grins at the revelation, powering him through his sign-off to the interview.

'Thanks, Ted. And see you all at Madison Square Garden tonight! I promise you all it will be one of my most explosive shows!'

Back in the car, Noah cannot stop laughing at the bad pun he had uttered on air that, of course, no one else in the world could have possibly understood, save for John K. Smiley, had he been listening. His laughter is cut short, however, when he realizes that his plans could be going awry in a rather crucial way.

'Where are we going?'

Jules looks at him, baffled by the question.

'To the MSG, boss. Sound check.'

'But I need to go back to the hotel first.'

Noah tries to sound calm as he says this but does not come close to pulling it off.

'If you've left something behind, I can . . .'

Noah cuts Jules off.

'We need to go back to the fucking hotel! Now!'

Jules looks at his watch and makes a few calculations.

'All right. You're the boss.'

Jules instructs the driver to turn around and head back to the hotel. He then turns back to his employer and says:

'We're cutting it close here, boss. How much time do you need up there?'

Jules probably thinks I'm going up there to whack off. His personal assistant is in fact the only person in Noah's life to have ever caught

137

onto the pop star's hotel porn habit, although Noah is completely unaware of this fact. This isn't down to any sort of intuitive ability Jules has; it's that he's the one who has to sign off on the final hotel bills.

'I need to run up, grab something quickly.'

Jules tries to read his employer's eyes and body language but can't pick up the signals. He lets it go as the car pulls up to the hotel and Noah gets out and runs towards the elevator.

When he gets inside his room, he dashes for the closet. Opening it, he hallucinates the silver case not being there for a split second, causing a rush of panic to hit him. Seeing the object in question the following moment helps Noah to breathe again. Respiratory troubles overcome, Noah slaps his knees a couple of time to psyche himself up, grabs the silver flight case and makes his way back to the car.

'Are you sure I can't put that in the trunk for you, boss?' Jules says, wondering what could possibly be in the case that would make Noah this covetous. Noah is holding it to his chest like it's a sick infant.

'I've got it, thank you, Jules.'

When they arrive at Madison Square Garden, Noah wants simply to head into the green room and think about how he is going to make the bomb operational, so he heads out of the car as soon as it comes to a standstill and starts heading in that direction.

'Boss,' Jules says to him, grabbing him by the sleeve. 'Stage is that way.'

Sound check. He'd completely forgotten about that in his single-mindedness.

'Right, I want to put some things down in the green room first.'

'Like that mysterious silver case you've been holding like it contains the crown jewels?' Jules asks.

'Keep being so clever and you'll be looking for another job soon, Jules.'

This line he throws at Jules out of the blue (panicking the poor PA) makes Noah realize as he says it that after tomorrow, Jules really will have to start looking for a new job anyhow. Dusting off his résumé, sending it out to companies. Which companies? What would Jules do as a follow-up job to the one he's had the past few years? Does wiping a pop star's ass count as a definable skill? Noah spends all of twenty seconds in the green room, simply looking for a place to put the silver case where it won't get moved or even touched by anyone, figures the foot space underneath the mirror should do the trick, and then departs for the stage.

The sound check is uneventful. Boring, as always, but no more so than usual. When it's finished, with Bobby the chief sound technician (been with Noah since the beginning – *shit, Bobby's going to have to find another gig too*) giving Noah the final thumbs up, the pop singer retreats back to his green room as quickly as his legs will carry him. When he gets inside, he locks the door behind him. His eyes dart around the room, searching for the silver flight case, Noah having now forgotten where he'd placed it. He looks seemingly everywhere without luck; he begins to panic. He is about to shout an obscenity loudly, something he always tries to avoid prior to a show for fear of blowing his voice, when he takes a seat in front of the mirror and then instantly finds what he had been looking for. The silver flight case is so close to his left leg he could have easily kicked it without moving his position. Hidden in plain sight. Noah laughs a little, a laugh of relief more than anything else. Now he will have to face what he had been putting off all day.

He opens up the case, slowly, feeling more nervous than he can remember ever being in the whole of his adult life. His palms sweaty, his limbs quivering all over, his vision slightly blurry; yet when he finally does set his eyes on the bomb, he feels a calm wash over him. All the fear and apprehension that had hung over the day to that point, even while he had been napping, evaporates instantly. He crouches down, looking at the device with wonder the only emotion.

Noah then carefully picks it up out of the casement and sets it down on the floor beside him. He begins to study it in detail, and as he does so his anxiety returns albeit for completely different reasons: now he is terrified by how little he can remember of Smiley's back porch explosives-related tutorials; how completely alien the device in front of him actually is. He knows, simply from this little initial investigation, that he has no chance whatsoever of arming the weapon prior to going on stage in a few hours' time. *No chance whatsoever.* A depression washes over Noah that is massive; huge, beyond anything he'd ever previously felt in his entire life. It is hopelessness beyond description. *I have to go on living. But I can't do that now. I'll have to kill myself some other way.* He thinks about alternatives: he could always simply take a bunch of pills. This doesn't improve his mood; he had the greatest suicide in the history of the world all lined up, and the only thing that was going to let him down in the end was his faulty memory. His insufficient brain.

'BOO!'

Noah leaps to his feet as this word is shouted at him. Pure terror runs through every neuron in his mind. As he collapses to the floor, holding his chest because it's the motion he finds comes naturally given the situation, Noah looks up to see the face of John K. Smiley peering at him.

'Gotcha.'

Smiley thinks his little prank is hilarious beyond belief. He can't stop laughing; that loud, horrible, drainpipe laugh of his, which had only ever gone off during the entirety of his existence in reaction to another human being's suffering. Noah comes to another revelation in a day full of them: his burning hatred of Smiley is at least thirty per cent down to that stupid laugh of his.

'Be quiet, John. One of my guys out there might think I'm being attacked and burst in and see this lying here in the goddamn open.'

Smiley realizes immediately that Noah probably does have a point on this count and forces himself to calm down.

'You have no idea how to make this sucker run, do you?'

Noah shakes his head, angry that Smiley, as always, is right.

'That's what I figured might happen, which is why I thought it best to come around and make sure you got it all working okay,' Smiley continues. Even though he's still angry at being scared in the manner that he was, a certain amount of relief that the plan could continue now that Smiley had shown up starts to settle in. He had already figured that one way or another he'd see Smiley one more time; thought that since the incident in Central Park, and the fact that John K. is now here to save the day in effect validates Noah's decision to tell him to fuck off earlier on. Smiley goes to the far corner of the room, picks up a large plastic bag and brings it back over to Noah.

'First off, happy death day, son.'

Noah opens the bag to find a collection of seemingly random books, such as *The Bell Jar* and *Steal This Book*. As he removes the books from the bag, he throws them onto a nearby couch. He's almost near the end when he sees a copy of the Koran.

'A Koran, John?'

'I figured you'd appreciate that.'

'What is this, reading material for the afterlife?'

'They were cluttering up my apartment. I figured you could go on stage with them, blow them to smithereens and do me a favour along the way.'

The preacher walks over to the explosive device and then picks it up a little less carefully than Noah thinks is prudent. He then goes one better and begins to wave it in Noah's face.

'I'll arm the son of a bitch and make it easy to detonate. Sound all right?'

'Great – now could you stop shaking it around, please?'

'You don't want to die just yet, is that it?'

'How the hell did you get past security anyhow?'

Smiley gives Noah his patented, smug, 'You're asking me, John K.

the genius, how I pulled off something you think of as difficult but to the likes of me is mere child's play?' face and leaves it at that. He then puts his head down and sets to work, pushing buttons, flicking little switches and generally setting up the weapon to operate. As he does this, Noah can't help but be transfixed by the man he'd worked so long and hard to leave behind at so many different points during his life, yet always found himself returning to.

Smiley was like a force of nature to Noah when he first came into contact with the mercurial man. Noah was seven, still enough of a believer in the infinite to think that perhaps Smiley was a guy who knew a thing or two about it. Noah's old man and Smiley were running some scam at the time that was based around insurance premiums that the boy was too young to understand. He didn't like thinking about his father's criminal activities much anyhow.

One day Smiley showed up at the Hastings' household (which was a trailer at the time) to discuss business with Abraham. He arrived twenty minutes early (a common Smiley trope), while Noah was still in the house (he was due to go to a friend's house for dinner than evening). Abraham was annoyed that Smiley had shown up while his boy was still in the house as it greatly increased the possibility of Noah's mother finding out about the meeting. Given Abraham had promised her he was done with Smiley after the last time he'd gotten them into trouble, this presented a big problem. He couldn't take it out on Smiley as John K. had himself well established as the alpha male in that relationship, so instead he did what came naturally and took it out on his son.

'What in God's name are you still doing hanging around here?' Abraham shouted at Noah. The boy was about to say sorry and then swiftly depart in the hopes of avoiding physical retribution when Smiley stepped in. With that drainpipe laugh and huge smile of his, the preacher-cum-scam artist walked towards Noah, picking him up in his arms as if he were a well-known uncle as opposed to a complete stranger.

'Don't take my reverse tardiness out on the poor young boy on my account, Abraham! What's your name again, son?'

'Noah.'

'Why that is a mighty fine name. Good work there, Abraham, giving your kin a good, solid name from the Old Testament.'

Abraham was annoyed about Noah being picked up like that – he considered any physical contact between men and boys that wasn't explicitly violent in nature, even a handshake, as suspect – but he couldn't help but smile at the compliment and forget about his grievance. Smiley was the one guy in the world he could never stay angry at, which was the chief unconscious reason that their relationship continued for as long as it did. It certainly wasn't their ability to make money from crime together, at which Smiley wasn't actually particularly talented. The only nefarious activity Smiley had ever made a monetary success of was getting his parishioners to give generously to whatever church he'd swindled his way into and then dip the till; quite literally the oldest trick in the book.

After this first embrace, Noah barely saw Smiley again for the next five and half years, Abraham having figured out in one of his few moments of real lucidity that his son and John K. could combine to form an alliance that probably wouldn't be altogether helpful to his standing with either of them. That was until that fateful evening when Noah's parents were out and Smiley dropped round and asked the boy if he wanted a beer, after the Gareth Gates piece of propaganda had been thrown against a wall in disgust. Conversation was tense early in the discussion, until Noah started to get a kick from the alcohol and opened up to Smiley about his atheism and the fishing trip incident involving Abraham dunking Noah into a lake headfirst. Noah expected Smiley to be either shocked or angry – defensive of his friend or disgusted by what Noah had told him about the domestic life of Abraham. Smiley was neither of these things. He simply took it all in and said solemnly:

'I'm glad you told me about this, son. Now I don't agree with your rejection of the Lord. But if you were my son, I would try and wear you down with my arguments, not with violence. After all, I know I'm on the right side of the debate, so why resort to anything but sense?'

Noah and Smiley each had another beer, and then another, then another. By that point, Noah was very drunk, unaccustomed as he was to alcohol in any quantity at that age. He became careless with his line of questioning as a result.

'Why do you hang out with my father when he's such a fucking deadbeat?'

Smiley found the question amusing and laughed out loud.

'You really hate your old man, don't you?'

'More than anything.'

'You'd like it if he was dead, wouldn't you?'

'Oh man, would I ever.'

A few weeks later, Abraham died of heart failure. In the week following his untimely, out of the blue demise, Noah felt constantly guilty about what he'd told Smiley the night of their Miller consumption. He thought that somehow wishing his father dead had caused it to become so. As much as he had hated his old man, he didn't want to be the one responsible for his passing.

Afterwards, Smiley moved further into Noah's life as a bizarre quasi-father figure. The years rolled by and Smiley was there; infrequently, but when he did show up in Noah's life again he was always happy to give Noah whatever he wanted. Time came when Noah said his goal was to become a singer and move to Los Angeles.

'I need a good demo,' he said to Smiley one day. 'And they cost about five thousand bucks.'

Smiley didn't even flinch. 'It's yours, son.'

The Smiley-financed demo was what Noah went armed with when he moved to Los Angeles, where he fed and sheltered himself via Smiley's new Hollywood digs. After he started to become a success, Noah expected Smiley, particularly given his background, to demand his cut of the 'investment' he'd made. Yet the first time he saw Noah after his big break – an appearance on a popular kids' programme, which led to a hit, indie single, which led to a record deal, all of this in the space of a week – it was strictly to congratulate him. To tell him how proud he was of Noah.

Smiley never asked for a cent, but he did have a tendency to hang around Noah's own new Hollywood house for extended periods of time – despite having his own place within five minutes' drive – which Noah jumped to the conclusion was the basis of the older man's support all along. For the record, it wasn't. Their relationship during this moment of early fame for Noah became less uncle-nephew and more like two male buddies who have known each other a long time and have all sorts of rivalries bubbling underneath the buddy-buddy surface. Smiley was drinking heavily then, which influenced Noah, who was struggling with his newfound stardom, to imbibe plenty of booze himself. It was around this time that Smiley and Noah rekindled their mutual interest in high-powered explosives.

'This shit is what the CIA use to blow the doors off panic rooms. Fits right into the thinnest of surfaces but could blow your leg clean off.'

Noah would ask him where he was getting the bombs from in LA – it had never occurred to Noah to ask about this back down south – after the third or fourth martini of the day, usually sometime during mid-morning. Smiley would be elusive on this subject, in sharp contrast to the technical information he was willing to share about the weapons, so Noah stopped asking where they came from after a short while.

Inevitably, Noah and Smiley had a big falling out. All of that alcohol mixed with weapons of mass destruction, not to mention the father issues Noah was still dealing with, made it only a matter of time. It happened over almost nothing, at least what would look like nothing to someone not immersed in their own burgeoning alcoholism. Noah accused Smiley of taking his last finger of vermouth and the older man lost his temper. Smiley was immediately thrown into exile, Noah kicking John K. out of the house and symbolically ending their friendship. Smiley, who had as one of his few redeeming features a desire to never stay where he wasn't wanted, did not demur and left without a fuss.

Opening chapter from the book, *The Noah Hastings Generation: Proceed with Caution* **by Slovakian intellectual Jadran Babic, published December 2021**

What becomes clear, when one examines the evidence available in an objective fashion, is that Noah Hastings was motivated not by Islamic fundamentalism but by some other force when he decided to terminate his life on June 16th, 2021, live on stage in front of thousands of baying children. What that other force was is difficult to say, although there are some clear clues available. I would like now to examine these alternate explanations for why Noah Hastings did as he did when he killed himself and those amongst his unfortunate *fanatikir,* those who like Icarus chose to fly too close to the sun and got burnt as a result. I think this an important exercise for many reasons, not least of which is intellectual clarity. However, I also think that the need to pin the blame on Islam comes from deep within the American psyche. This blind spot is obscuring the truth.

First, we must think about the paraphernalia discovered in both the wreckage of the backstage area after the incident, as well as what was found in Hastings' hotel room. The backstage portion of Madison Square Garden was not so badly hit. No one in this area died, as a for instance, but there were some bad injuries, and the 'green room' where Hastings would have spent his last few moments out of the public eye sustained some minor damage but was left mostly intact. This dressing room is interesting mostly because it is cluttered with materials, many of which are conflicting in their ideological bent, much more so than you would expect a 'normal' pop star's green room to ideologically contain. I put 'normal' in quotations owing to the fact that there isn't such a thing as an average pop phenomenon, pretty much by definition, but nonetheless there are some cultural and logical norms that can be applied. Hastings would not have spent a great deal of time in this room before the concert and he would have known beforehand, given what he was planning to do, that the space would be scoured for clues afterwards as a *tatort*. Thus, it is odd that there is such a wide range of different reading material. Unless, of course, Noah Hastings was much cleverer than anyone suspected and carefully laid out the room in order to provide a litany of red herrings. I will go through a partial list: a copy of the Bible; a copy of the Koran; a copy of *Mein Kampf*; a book of William Blake poems; several David Foster Wallace novels; some old, borderline racist comic books from the Second World War; a book about alchemy, reputedly from the Middle Ages; *Men are from Mars, Women are from Venus;* some Harry Potter novels.

What can we tell from this collection of literature? Absolutely nothing, obviously, except to try and second-guess Noah Hastings' motivation for laying out the room with such eclectic items. In common parlance, we are expected to believe from the fact that he had a copy of the Koran that Noah Hastings was inspired by fundamentalist Islam when he murdered those ninety-one children in New York City. Thus far, no other evidence has been brought to light publicly. What the Federal Bureau of Investigation will say is that they have more evidence; confidential information that they cannot release to the public. This is what the American industrial/military complex always has to say for itself. So far, they have had little to worry about politically: pollsters tell us all we need to know about the depth of conviction the American public has when it comes to Islam as MSG bombing motivation. It is about eighty-five per cent at present, despite increasing doubt being sowed amongst the cognoscenti.

What is remarkable in this context is how clear the proof against the Muslim motivation actually is when examined objectively. The

Los Angeles imam, who himself has said that he had not been in touch with Hastings for several years up until they spoke face to face on the day of the bombing itself (which is admittedly an unsettling coincidence), also has said clearly that under his aegis Noah Hastings never became a Muslim, never mind being primarily motivated by his faith in the religion. The proof linking Hastings to Islam, and with this, Islam to the terrible crime perpetrated at the ice hockey arena in New York on June 16th, 2021, seems flaky at best when everything the imam has said is taken into consideration. The way this is dismissed within the United States' collective consciousness is by assuming that the imam is lying, simply covering his tracks, helped by the fact that the imam is now being held in federal custody under the Patriot Act, his relationship with Noah Hastings having finally been deemed latently criminal in nature (*Editor's note: this book was written while Amir Elahi was still being held in custody by the FBI*). By the bounds of normal jihadist behaviour, this would be odd practice; fundamentalist terrorists are usually quick to take the blame/credit for such atrocities. Indeed, it makes little sense from a terrorist point of view to perpetrate such things without letting people know, clearly and uncategorically, who did what and why.

Coming back to the eighty-five percent *bestätigen* figure once more: this is an astonishing number. The fact that the narrative in question has been put forward by the apparatus of the state isn't enough of an explanation. A huge number of Americans are suspicious of what their government says and yet even this constituency has been convinced on the matter. America is the land of the conspiracy theories and yet here we are: a Slovakian debunker of conspiracy theories is suggesting that the American government may have deliberately misled its people into a froth about Islam. Of course, there are indeed some voices in America suggesting the Islamic angle is, as they say, 'a stitch-up'. However, they are from the usual, unreliable channels: far-right groups, conspiracy theory mavens, anti-Semitic militia men, supermarket tabloids. Why are

149

none of the usual mainstream American antennae twitching? (*Editor's note: the final text of this book was drafted both before Nina Hargreaves' Washington Sun article about John K. Smiley was published, and her subsequent parting from said newspaper was actioned.*)

It is possible that the crime, like the events of September 11th, 2001, touched something deep within the American psyche, and that an explanation – whatever explanation – needed to be grasped as soon as possible. The thought that this was simply the nihilistic act of a single individual would have been too much to bear; it had to have been ideological, and of course, sprung from an ideology that is alien to the American mainstream. Islam had been tried before and worked; the higher echelons of the American state did not have to 'reinvent the wheel', nor attempt anything which might backfire on them. Islamophobia lay dormant in the population; one needed only to *leuchtet das spiel* for the fire to rage out of control once again. This seems to me to be at least a partial explanation for the FBI press release of June 26th, 2021 – but only a partial one.

The other element can perhaps be found in the countervailing *erklärung* of what happened on June 16th, 2021 in New York City. It is a story that is told in whispers and is nowhere near mainstream thinking or even the more outré portions of the mainstream press (*Editor's note: see previous note on this text pre-dating the Nina Hargreaves article*). It postulates that Noah Hastings' motivation for killing himself and his fans at Madison Square Garden that evening was fundamentalist Christianity, not Islam, and that another figure from Noah Hastings' past, an obscure preacher named John K. Smiley, was the prime motivator and architect of the whole plan.

Smiley is so obscure that even his actual existence has not yet been verified. There does seem to be enough circumstantial evidence however to suggest that a person calling himself by this name played a major role in Hastings' life on and off for many years. The story goes: Smiley was a friend of Noah's father, Abraham Hastings, who of course was a verifiably real person who was a Baptist preacher himself until he was found out to be a con man and sent to prison. Hastings' father had many sketchy associates, several of whom worked under pseudonyms; it might be that John K. Smiley is the *nom de guerre* of one of these former allies. According to these whispered rumours, Smiley was seen with Hastings in Central Park the day of the bombing. Some witnesses seem to put Smiley at Madison Square Garden, shortly before the bomb went off during the concert as well. Again, it needs to be mentioned how unsubstantiated any of this information is. However, it is as proven in the public sphere as the Islamic fundamentalism theory, so worth taking with the same level of intellectual seriousness.

This leads me to another problem closely linked with the Noah Hastings bombing: that of our limited technological capabilities in investigating something of this nature when placed alongside the technology we already live with day to day. A pop star has the ability to strap a bomb to himself and kill almost one hundred people, and yet our means for discovering who or what was behind this atrocity remain rooted in the nineteenth century. The scouting around for artefacts; the conclusions made by tenuous association; fingerprinting has not even been necessary to arrive at the conclusions that the American state apparatus has done.

What this all leads me to is what I consider to be the most *tiefgründig* question facing the human race: what is the nth degree of technological advancement? In other words, what is the ultimate purpose of *technologischen Fortschritt*? When will the road, so to speak, end? I believe that the ultimate *zweck*, both unconsciously and consciously, is to extend human life indefinitely. But that is impossible, you will say. This is only true if you choose to narrowly define what human life contains. If you think about human life being extended eternally and include in your definition of such a thing as *Roboterlebensformen* that have successfully absorbed all that humanity contains and are in a way more human than real humans, then I think this is the ultimate aim of our thirst for creating ever greater forms of technology.

I have digressed far too much here: back to my original conceit. We have no idea why Noah Hastings killed himself and all those children on June 16th, 2021. We will almost certainly never know. But it is useless to go on convincing ourselves that what we have obtained thus far is the whole of truth on the matter.

Throughout the course of this book, I will dig as deep as I can do to discover the underlying truth behind the Noah Hastings bombing.

'Why the John K. Smiley myth is gaining currency', by Joseph Cummings, from *Scope* magazine, January 2022 edition

As American culture enters a new phase in the aftermath of the Hastings bombing, we see an inversion of the Kubler-Ross model taking place before us. We have gone through the stages of anger, bargaining and even acceptance already. We now find ourselves back at what should technically be stage one: denial.

While we have gotten no nearer to understanding the exact details of how and with whom Noah Hastings did what he did on the night of June 16th at Madison Square Garden in the half-year since the incident took place, we seemed to at least have answered why it happened. Yet in the void left by the admittedly poor FBI investigation into the matter, some have now decided to question even that.

A distinct group of people wish to deny the link between the Hastings bombing and Islamist terrorism for socio-political reasons which are perfectly understandable. The wave of Islamophobia that has unfurled across America over the preceding six months has been a wearying spectacle to behold. Others wish to deny the link simply on the basis of no further evidence coming to light, citing habeas corpus. To be fair to this latter group, the proof that does seem to materialize in the investigation so far vanishes as quickly as it arrives, leading understandably to frustration and talk of conspiracy.

For all that, it is still worth remembering for a moment how stories involving John K. Smiley were consigned either to the tabloids or far-right fanzines and websites only a matter of a few weeks ago.

What changed this dynamic was the Nina Hargreaves scandal, in which the *Washington Telegraph* carried out the cultural equivalent of throwing water onto an oil fire. This had the effect of moving the Smiley conspiracy theory squarely into mainstream journalism.

The way this has happened is sociologically fascinating. The lack of further evidence telling us definitively how and why Noah Hastings was motivated by fundamentalist Islamism in committing the atrocity at the MSG led to a massive build-up of tension within the mainstream media over the months since the bombing occurred. The Hargreaves firing was when this rigidity came undone; when the American media reached a breaking point. The journalists and their magnate overlords needed to come up with something, anything of substance; they had to provide some real news on the story for a change. As the Hargreaves firing from the *Telegraph* became about free speech – and more importantly, about direct attacks on the livelihoods of newspaper journalists, a group of people newspaper journalists are always keen to protect – it became acceptable to write about the previously off-limits topic of the John K. Smiley conspiracy theory as if it were not 'fake news'. Journalists wanted to write about Smiley to show solidarity with the fired Hargreaves, in other words.

Given its centrality in taking the Hastings bombing narrative to a new and scary place, it is worth noting the facts of the matter. Sources at the *Washington Telegraph* have told me that while the official reason given for Nina Hargreaves being let go by the paper was her expenses, the de facto cause had more to do with the suspicion that a quote in her article from December 4th was invented or at least embellished. In Hargreaves' piece, there is an extended quote from a Reverend William Gene who says that he recalls Abraham Hastings had an acquaintance named Smiley. Yet a follow-up with Reverend Gene by the *Telegraph* after the December 4th article had already gone to press revealed that he had been hospitalized for dementia four years prior to the interview last month with Hargreaves, and that doctors at the home in which he resides wondered whether it would have been technically possible for Reverend Gene to have been as lucid as the transcription in the Hargreaves article indicates. Even if Reverend Gene had somehow been able to say exactly what he is quoted as saying in the article, Hargreaves at no point in the piece makes note of the fact that Reverend Gene is being treated for senility. One is given the distinct impression in the text of the article that he is still a practising Baptist preacher, in fact. Whatever the validity of the quote, she should have made it clearer who exactly the source was and why his recounting of history may reasonably be called into question.

It is one thing for all of the newspapers in the land to find themselves unable to get an interview with a particular individual. It is another thing altogether when the combined might of serious American journalism cannot even fully verify the existence of said individual. Yet that is where we are with John K. Smiley. Poring over the history as revealed by Nina Hargreaves and others is useful in demonstrating this.

Abraham Hastings, Noah's father, was in prison twice. The stint during which he supposedly met John K. Smiley was the first one, when Abraham was twenty-three years of age. There is no record of a John Smiley serving time at the Louisiana State Penitentiary when Abraham Hastings was incarcerated there. In fact, there has never been a prisoner in the entire state of Louisiana since records began named John Smiley. Obviously Smiley could be an alias – and this has been discussed in the better articles on the subject – yet Louisiana state police have no record of any crime being investigated, never mind brought to a trial resulting in conviction, by anyone using that pseudonym either.

There was a Jeremiah Samson who served time at the same institution as Abraham Hastings when the latter was in his twenties. The two men were even linked together in a series of investigated yet unsolved crimes following this period. As a result of this, several journalists have offered the theory that Jeremiah Samson is John K. Smiley. There is one problem with this thesis, at least in so far as the Noah Hastings bombing goes: Jeremiah Samson has been dead for six years. This fact is an easily verifiable one. That portions of the American mainstream media have chosen to ignore it or not bothered to look it up suggests that either a mass laziness has settled into journalism all of a sudden or there is a deep-seated need to find an alternative version of events.

The myth of the roving southern man who is able to live in the shadows and yet pop up at the right moment to strike when and where we are vulnerable is an old one, its roots in American culture running deep. According to the tabloid narrative that has now bled into the mainstream like a game of Folding Story, this Smiley character was supposed to have had a huge influence on Noah Hastings until something happened to make them fall out sometime before Noah reached adulthood. However, the two reconciled at some point, leading to 'John K.' somehow being behind the rise of Hastings' fame (parallels with the Satan of blues lore), funding the budding star's early demos and using his connections to get his songs to the 'right people'. Why a southern Baptist preacher would have a load of LA music industry insider contacts is what confuses me most about this part of the construct.

Years later, burnt out and wishing he could escape from his own fame, Noah Hastings is visited again by the devil called Smiley. The preacher calls in his favour, holding a bomb in his hand as he does so. Hastings, having made that promise all those years ago, has no choice but to comply.

Until the FBI can make a definitive breakthrough in their investigation into the Hastings bombing, I believe we may have to suffer through a mini-epoch of John K. Smiley stories. We should probably actually try and enjoy this, for what comes next is bound to be ugly. I predict the investigation will eventually lead back to Amir Elahi in one way or another, and a lid will be lifted on a programme of inter-American jihadism that will be like nothing we have ever previously heard about. The wave of Islamophobia we have been experiencing over the last six months may come to resemble a few capillary waves prior to the tsunami ahead. At least then we will have moved from denial to anger and from there perhaps bargaining and depression can be moved through quickly enough to get to where America needs to be desperately: in a place where acceptance of the truth is possible.

The FBI confirm the arrest of Jeremiah Samson, aka John K. Smiley, in connection with the Noah Hastings' bombing – March 19th, 2022

MACON, GA (AP) – The FBI have today arrested a man in connection with the Noah Hastings bombing of last year. The suspect, Jeremiah Samson, occasionally known to friends and associates as John K. Smiley, was arrested outside of a bar located on Macon, Georgia's Mulberry Street. The Bureau had been investigating Mr Samson for several months prior to making the arrest in connection with the incident that took place on June 16th, 2021, in which ninety-two people perished at Madison Square Garden during a pop concert.

Mr Samson has been charged with ninety-two counts of conspiracy to murder, terrorism, and first-degree murder. He is also accused of having supplied the weapon which Noah Hastings later detonated during his concert on June 16th, 2021, a crime which carries with it a separate charge.

Mr Samson is being held at Arlington, Virginia's military prison while awaiting trial.

A formal statement from Mr Smiley, upon his arrest, read:

'I admit fully to my involvement in the Noah Hastings bombing which took place in New York City on June 16th of last year. I both supplied the weapon and convinced Mr Hastings to participate in the incident. I did this because I wanted to wake America up from the sin perpetuated through popular music of the kind sung by the late Mr Hastings. I hope through this statement to inspire more of my Christian brothers to take up similar acts in the name of our Lord, Jesus Christ. Only through acts which help people see the Satanic trap the United States of America is falling into can we bring the American people back into the light.'

It has not been clarified yet whether or not Mr Samson's statement can be taken to be a confession in the legal sense, but under Miranda it can be used against him during his trial.

It has been speculated that one of the chief reasons why Mr Samson may have been able to evade arrest for such an extended period of time is that due to either administrative error or some kind of inside internal record tampering, he had been pronounced dead by the state of Louisiana on August 16th, 2015. A separate FBI investigation will be launched to look into how this error in record keeping occurred.

The FBI's statement on the arrest of Mr Samson, which preceded the suspect's own statement, reads as follows:

'Today we have apprehended the chief suspect in the Noah Hastings' New York bombing incident, Jeremiah Samson, in Macon, Georgia. Mr Samson has been charged with ninety-two counts of conspiracy to murder as well as first-degree murder, in addition to several terrorism felonies. He will be held at Arlington's military prison until trial. He is also alleged to have supplied the weapon which caused the catastrophe on June 16th, 2021 and a separate charge in relation to this will be allocated to Mr Samson at a later date, once a full investigation into the matter has been completed. The FBI have been monitoring the suspect for several months and the Bureau was able to piece together Mr Samson's alleged involvement in the events leading up to the bombing of June 16th of last year and on the day of the bombing itself. More details will be put forth from our office over the coming days and weeks.'

The arrest of Mr Samson and his subsequent statement dramatically reverses the assumptions made up until now about Noah

159

Hastings' motivation in carrying out the actions of June 16th, 2021 at Madison Square Garden. Namely the factor that Islam played in the bombing, which now appears to be in serious doubt. The White House has declined to comment on the arrest.

'The idea that this is now Christianity's fault is absurd', by Patricia McShay, an article from the website *Bratbrey*, published March 20th, 2022

The liberals, I have got to hand it to them, they never do miss a trick. Jeremiah Samson was charged as a major co-conspirator in the Noah Hastings bombing yesterday, and already here they come, saying that we should blame not only Christianity, but every Christian in the world for what happened at Madison Square Garden nine months ago. As if, simply because someone says they did something horrible in the name of a religion, that automatically means that the religion itself is at fault for what happened. What warped logic.

After almost a year now of constantly saying that Islam shouldn't be blamed for the Noah Hastings bombing on the basis of what was supposed at the time to be the influence of Islam, liberals turn around and hypocritically want to blame Christianity for the whole thing. They make me sick. Their hypocrisy should discount them from being taken seriously by any sane individual.

How exactly is the motivation of one demented individual, or even a small group of disturbed people, supposed to represent the way in which billions of people around the world view their own faith? Just because Jeremiah Samson thinks that his version of Christianity compels him to murder innocent people does not in any way reflect upon what most decent Christians think at all. Notice how we don't have millions of Christians going around creating terrorist atrocities? A few bad apples do not reflect on the quality of the barrel.

God, I hate liberals. Really hate them. So many of them are all over social media today, smug as ever. They can't see that there is a fundamental difference between Islam and Christianity, can they? That even if there were say, ten Jeremiah Samson-type figures going around the country talking about killing people in the name of Christianity, that wouldn't be anywhere near as bad as one Muslim doing the same thing. Can you not see the difference, liberal cucktards?

Jesus preached love. Mohammed preached hate. Jesus told his followers to give up all of their possessions and follow him into oblivion. Mohammed told his followers to arm themselves to the teeth and invade Europe. Jeremiah Samson is simply confused about what Christianity is; the guys who carried out 9/11 on the other hand, they were following the teachings of the Koran to the letter. Anyone who can't see that is a serious liberal dongpiece.

That should be it, case closed, but because the internet is teeming with pretentious liberal merkins today, I need to make this a slam dunk here.

There are so many examples of hateful crap in the Koran, I'm not going to waste your time on it. Libtards say the Bible is just as bad. Really? The worst thing I could find in the Bible is this, from Deuteronomy, Chapter 13:

'If your own brother, or your son or daughter, or the wife you love, or your closest friend secretly entices you, saying, "Let us go and worship other gods" do not yield to them or listen to them. Show them no pity. Do not spare them or shield them. You must certainly put them to death. Your hand must be the first in putting them to death, and then the hands of all the people. Stone them to death, because they tried to turn you away from the Lord your God, who brought you out of Egypt, out of the land of slavery.'

The difference between the two religions should be clear for all reasonable people to see.

'What's the difference between murder in the name of Islam and murder in the name of Jesus?', Julia Worthy, from *The Tribeca Taddler* magazine, April 2022 edition

Is it too off the wall to suggest a conspiracy to fool the American people has been witnessed? The flavour of the reveal that radical Islam had played no part whatsoever in the Hastings bombing following the arrest of the supposedly mythical John K. Smiley has almost entirely been one of 'nothing to see here, folks' from the mainstream press. Worse, there have been overtones of cultural relativity in spades through all of this over the past couple of weeks. Underneath every article discussing the John K. Smiley arrest is the subliminal notion that somehow a terrorist atrocity done in the name of Jesus is more palatable than one done in the name of Mohammed.

Smiley himself has said, in no uncertain terms during one of his innumerable dealings with the press since his arrest, that what motivated him to commit his part in the horrible crime perpetrated on June 16th of last year was his Christian faith, and furthermore that the children who bought Hastings' music and attended his concerts needed to 'die so that they may cleanse their souls of the sin that has infected them'. To summarize, this man has taken part in the murder of almost one hundred innocent children, has said without reserve that his inspiration was Christianity, and what follows? A cry against the horrible faith that was the motivation for this deed? The harassment of fundamentalist

Christians and their churches to be more vocal in decrying this episode, or at least be vigilant against an oncoming onslaught of abuse?

I've heard not a peep from anyone in the American media about whether the role of Christianity in American life should be questioned in light of John K. Smiley's fundamentalist outpourings, never mind turning around and suggesting that Christianity is a vile, hate-filled religion that should be demonized. As it happens, I don't think that Christianity is any of those things I just mentioned either, nor do I believe it should now be held to account in some way. But you only have to recall how hatred of Islam became de rigueur in American life after it was announced by the FBI that they believed (erroneously as it turned out) that radical Islam was the main motivation for the Hastings bombing. I have noted the lack of redress coming the way of Muslims around the fact that the entirety of American society put them up for trial based on what turned out to be completely fallacious reasoning. It seems to me like this is the least that should be coming their way.

I am an atheist, so to me Christianity and Islam are very similar. Both Abrahamic religions; both based on books with some nice things to say about how human beings should behave towards one another; both religions' books are also filled with gory, horrible stuff like incest, paedophilia and genocide. As a result, I find it confusing when at one point in time a terrible crime is pinned on one of these religions (on what turned out to be circumstantial and indeed, false evidence) and we are then told endlessly about how this ideology is the spawn of Satan, the greatest risk to American prosperity since Stalin, etc. Then when it turns out the other religion was actually to blame no one says anything about it at all.

Obviously, simply because a Christian preacher, who claims that Christianity caused him to murder, goes ahead and kills hundreds of children in the name of Jesus that does not mean that Christianity and indeed ordinary Christians are to blame. Of course not. That would be like blaming all of Islam and every single one of the world's 1.4 billion Muslims for the actions of one pop star who was supposedly influenced by the Koran. Right?

'The Double Standard' by Shaheen Dasti, a noted conservative writer, thinker and campaigner – article on *Bratbrey*, June 2022

As many of you who are aware of my work will already know, I'm not a big believer in the 'apology culture' that pervades America these days. I would enjoy it more, for instance, if when politicians screwed up they'd turn around, do the decent thing and quit. As opposed to doing what they usually do, which is going on TV and blubbing about how sorry they are in a transparent attempt to keep their government paycheck.

However, sometimes something in the way of an apology is not only right, but absolutely essential. The current moment is a case in point. Last June, the FBI laid the blame for a horrific event that took place in New York City several days beforehand at the feet of Islamic extremism. It turned out that it was not jihadism that was the motivation behind the attack, but rather fundamentalist Christianity in the form of a corrupt, fallen Baptist preacher known as John K. Smiley. For nine months post-June 16th, physical attacks on Muslim citizens of our great land went up by an astonishing 462%. Islam itself, and its role in American life, was severely questioned. Given all of this, it would be nice for the president to make an apology to all of the USA's twenty million Muslims. Scratch that, I think such a thing is owed to us.

As many of you out there within Republican circles who know me will already be aware of, this is not something I ask lightly. I am a conservative, pragmatic individual who does not 'trade on race' as some are (rightly) accused of. There is nothing tokenistic in what I request here today. I have on many occasions said that Muslims in this country must do more to fit in; that they must do more to integrate. That while there is no need to convert to Christianity, we as Muslims must be aware that America is a Christian country and we must respect that. But it is difficult for me to go on imploring my fellow Muslims that America is a land of equality when jihadism is decried for causing the death of almost a hundred people, yet when it turns out to be fundamentalist Christianity that was the culprit, a mysterious double standard creeps in.

If we are to live together in peace and harmony, which is the fundamental idea of America that our forefathers envisioned, then we must not let one faith be dominant over all the rest to the extent that it begins to involve persecution of said followers of any faith that is not the dominant one. Wasn't this the reason the pilgrims hopped on the *Mayflower* and sailed to Plymouth Rock in the first place? During the time in which we all believed that fundamentalist Islam was thought to be the motivation behind the Noah Hastings bombing in New York City, I was loudest amongst American Muslims, I believe, in denouncing jihadism. In calling out what I saw as a perversion of my own religion. Now that it has been revealed that fundamentalist Christianity was the motivation for the same crime, I have to wonder where are the pastors, the priests, the reverends and the bishops, flooding the airwaves to denounce what is surely a perversion of their religion? For they cannot possibly believe that a terrorist act committed in the name of Christ is somehow less atrocious than one committed in the name of Mohammed. Can they?

When we believed the Hastings atrocity was motivated by Islam, I said that all of us, every American, be they Muslim or otherwise, must stand up and be counted. What happened in New York on June 16th, 2021 was a horrible act with no possible equivocation. Why are we hearing nothing from the Christian community now that it has been shown to be an act motivated by their faith instead of another?

Take the innocent imam, Mr Elahi, who had been arrested late last year in connection with the incident at Madison Square Garden. He was detained without trial, under laws I myself had argued in the past were necessary to deal with the threat America faced from jihadist terrorists. Even he has not to date been formally apologized to or even publicly cleared of any wrongdoing. The FBI simply released him without charge (for what was a second time, in fact) and have since refused any press enquires on the matter. I wanted to interview him on my show a few weeks ago and was told by him personally that he could not legally discuss the matter. If Mr Elahi has had his silence bought, then while I cannot blame him, I can certainly mourn the loss of an opportunity to shed some light on what was clearly a miscarriage of justice.

I have long told my fellow Muslims that the country they live in, what is undoubtedly the greatest nation in the history of all mankind, is one of blind justice, of equal opportunity. One in which a Muslim boy whose father came from the streets of Karachi to America with only a few cents in his pocket can become a millionaire, respected within the supposedly 'dominated by whites' Republican Party. But now, for the first time in my life, I am unsure of the ethics of this great nation. It is an uncomfortable place for me to be. I desperately want to hear that apology from my president, the FBI and from members of my own party who have spoken out of turn about my faith. I feel I may be waiting a long time for such a thing, if not for the rest of time. Someone please prove me wrong.

June 16th, part five ('We're on, boss')

Multiple beads of sweat trickle down John K. Smiley's face as he applies the finishing touches to both the device and Noah's stage costume, an outfit vitally needed to obscure the device from view before it can be detonated.

'You're going to knock 'em dead, son. Literally!'

They both laugh at this quip, much louder and longer than they should have given the quality of the comment. Noah gets a sudden inspiration as he begins to calm down again.

'I've always meant to ask you something, John.'

'I think now's your last chance, son.'

'Why have you always done everything you've ever done for me? I mean, it can't be because of my old man. You guys seemed like you were growing apart around the time that he died. Why have you always treated me like I was, I don't know . . .'

'My own son? I guess because that's the way I've always seen you, Noah. I have a couple of confessions to make. One, and I've never revealed to this to another man: I'm not physically able to have children. I found that out when I was about twenty-two and my first wife Mabel and I had been trying for some time. That hit me pretty hard, knowing I'd never have a boy of my own. Then when I met you, I don't know, I guess something maternally kicked in.'

'I think you mean paternally?'

There is a pause. It seems like Smiley is gathering his thoughts, which is strange to Noah since he'd never seen Smiley in anything that could pass as a contemplative mood before, ever.

'You intimated that you had two confessions to make,' Noah

finally says. Smiley pauses for a moment and then emerges from himself, all confidence.

'I killed your father.'

Noah rather predictably pauses to take this in.

'Stop fucking around,' Noah says.

'I mean it, son. I poisoned him.'

Another pause.

'What is this, John?'

'It's the truth.'

'The old man died of heart failure.'

'Brought on by a type of rare toxicant called psyedelidin-480. Extremely difficult to get outside of military circles. Untraceable by conventional police means. Luckily, I had a few army guys who owed me a favour.'

Noah weighs all this up. It is possible that Smiley is lying, simply trying to get his last head-fuck in while he can. Yet it would also make complete sense if he was telling the truth; Smiley as a murderer is completely believable, after all. Noah eventually settles on the answer: it makes no difference whatsoever if Smiley killed his father or if his old pa died from natural causes. Noah hated his dad and he hates Smiley too. If Smiley killed his father, well, Noah was about to ruin Smiley's life, in a roundabout sort of a way. So, everything is about to come good, as far as Noah sees it.

'Why did you do it?' Noah asks out of pure curiosity.

'You asked me to.'

'When?'

'That first drink we had together, you remember? You told me you hated him and wished he were dead.'

Noah pauses to take this in. The guilt he felt after his father died was well grounded after all. Noah did kill him, in an odd sort of a way.

'Why would that be enough for you to have gone and done something like that? I mean, that was like, the first real conversation we ever had.'

170

'I don't know how to put this . . . you're the only person besides myself I've ever actually cared about. I'm not sure why, not sure how, but that's the truth of it. I'm what you might call, I guess, a psychopath, or a sociopath. I never really understood the difference, but I'm definitely one of those. No empathy, no feeling for others. Except you, Noah. I care about you. Like I say, I don't know why, but I do.'

'What about God?'

'What about him?'

'Don't you care about God?'

'You were always right about that one. There is no God.'

'Why did you get me this bomb to kill myself with if you care about me that much?'

'For the same reason I killed your old man: because you asked me to.'

'That's it? You don't even want to try and talk me out of it?'

'Do you want me to talk you out of it?'

'I don't know.'

That was real honesty on Noah's part.

'Look, if you don't want to do it, don't do it.'

'I want to do it. I need to do it. I don't get how . . . if you care about me so much, why are you willing to help me kill myself?'

Smiley stands up and paces a bit. He then turns around and looks up at Noah, square in the eye.

'Because I want you to do whatever it is you want to do in this life, son. That's why I gave you the money for that demo tape all those years back; why I moved out to Los Angeles so's you'd have a place to work from when you got there, and someone to support you both financially and emotionally. It isn't my place to talk you towards one thing or another. With everyone else in the world, I manipulate, I con; I try and get people to do what I want 'em to. And I don't want you to die, Noah. I sincerely don't. I'll miss you more than you could ever know, even though we ain't been speaking all that much since you kicked me out of your place that one time.'

171

'Sorry about that, by the way. I was so fucking precious about that vermouth. I'm sorry about that, John.'

As Noah apologizes for the vermouth incident all those years ago, he finds he at least half means it. In spite of himself, Noah feels the hatred he has towards Smiley loosen a little. To say he hates Smiley in the pure way he consciously thinks he does is too simplistic anyhow. His feelings towards Smiley are actually much more complex than he can possibly come to grips with. They are intertwined with too many other things: his feelings for his father, for Christianity, towards his whole childhood. Smiley is too connected to too many moving parts in his life.

'No need to say sorry, son. You did what you thought was right. And I needed a kick up the ass anyhow. I was starting to take advantage of your hospitality; to treat you like I treat everyone else.'

'You don't want me to do this tonight. The bomb and all that, I mean.'

'Like I said, I want you to do whatever it is you want to do.'

'But you personally would rather I didn't.'

'Once you're gone, Noah, that's it. I'm back to not caring about a soul in the world. So, no, I'd personally prefer you remained in one piece myself.'

Noah finds himself crying. In other words, he thinks about having a weep only to discover that he is already in the midst of one.

'I'm not going to do this then.'

Smiley looks as ashen-faced and as serious as Noah had ever seen him look after the pop singer announces his sudden change of heart. Smiley turns away from Noah for a moment to stare down at his hands and then back up towards his former amanuenses to say:

'Don't be a jackass, son. Go with your heart and don't worry about this old fool right here. I know that at least part of the reason you're doing all of this, the way you're doing it too, is because you want to implicate me in the whole thing.'

This comment genuinely takes Noah by surprise. At least for a moment; he quickly realizes that Smiley not figuring out what he had been planning was foolhardy. *Does he know I hate him too? Probably. Most likely the whole reason he cares about me, perversely enough.*

'How did you figure that one out?'

'It's obvious enough. Why ask me to get involved?'

'Because you're the only terrorist I know?'

'For a start, that's not exactly true, is it? What about them neo-Nazis you used to hang around with a few years back?'

'They hate me. I threw them out of my house.'

'You threw me out of your house too, man!'

They both laugh for a brief moment.

'Why did you bring that bomb to my hotel room if you think the whole thing is about me attaching you to what I'm about to do?'

'Maybe I want to be impregnated. You ever think about that?'

'I think you mean implicated, John.'

Noah spots the trigger device hanging off the side of the weapon; the only portion of the device that is visible. Smiley's eyes go to the same place. He walks back over to Noah and crouches down in front of him.

'Right, this baby you're looking at now is what you want to cradle like a new born. You'll have to press the ignition button pretty dang hard in the usual circumstances – but you'd be amazed what a little slip can do. Just remember, son, you have a real piece of hardware strapped to your back, and that little red button is rigged to make it all go boom. That thing taped to your chest right now could take out a whole Manhattan tower block.'

'Got it.'

The two men then proceed to hang out together in that small room for the following forty-five minutes or so, saying little to one another, everything that needed to be said having already been said. Smiley gets up every so often to take a drink from the mini-bar while Noah tries to move around as little as possible for fear of setting off the device. Noah drinks only sparkling water – even during his worst boozing days he never drank before a show and he isn't about to start now. Eventually a knock comes on the door. It is Noah's usual signal from Jules that they are now ten minutes from show time. Smiley gets up from his chair and opens the door to go.

'I can't look at you again, Noah, so this is it, goodbye. I'll always love you, son.'

Smiley then leaves, shutting the door behind him. Noah takes a deep breath, then another, then another. He waits a few more seconds, until he can be sure that John K. really was gone and that the two of them wouldn't catch another glimpse of each other. He then sets to work.

Since he had formulated his plan to take his own life and the lives of any of his fans who happened to be in bomb range the previous day while sitting with Andy in economy class, a few ideas had started to emerge in Noah's mind around the little details. He figured out that the green room area would be heavily scoured for clues as to his motivation, and he had come to the conclusion that being as cheeky as possible would be ideal. Part of this plan hinged to some degree on Noah going to a bookshop and buying the necessary materials for the job, but he had in the end only brought with him the copy of *Mein Kampf* that Eva had given to him as a birthday present and the Bible from the hotel room. However, Smiley, as per usual, has saved the day. He takes the books out of the bag Smiley had brought and begins spreading them over the room, as if he was building an art installation. They are a bizarre, seemingly random collection of books; *all the better then*.

Job done, Noah decides to have one last stroll around the backstage area before the show. The moment he leaves the green room, however, the soon to be ex-pop star is semi-accosted by a pair of female fans who had somehow got backstage via some dreadful radio contest and slipped free of their escort.

'Oh gosh, Mr Hastings, my sister is so your biggest fan ever. I love you too, don't get me wrong, but my sister, man, she really loves you, if you catch my drift.'

Noah looks over at the sibling of the girl who had given him this oratory. Her sister had not been exaggerating for effect: the girl is frozen by love, seized by it almost. She can say nothing, only look unblinkingly at the object she craves with all her heart that is mere footsteps away, her face contorted by the strength of her feelings and of her disbelief at the proximity of her beloved. Noah looks at the girl and decides quickly what he has to do next. He slowly approaches her, almost shuffling his face up to hers until their noses are practically touching. As he creeps towards her, the girl's face registers an odd mixture of sexual desire, childish joy, and sheer terror. As the first of Noah's breaths to fall under her nostrils are inhaled by the hysterical fan, she appears to have an orgasm, at least to Noah. He then puts the cherry on top: he kisses the girl on the lips. Within milliseconds she has passed out, completely cold. As he watches her fall away from him, Noah thinks seriously for the first time in almost an hour about what was to happen that evening, the event that only he and John K. Smiley currently knew about, the one which would be remembered throughout the ages by every human being set to live forever more. *Enjoy it all now, my pretty. You'll be dead in a few hours' time.* Noah then laughs to himself, a little giggle that escapes. It is caused mainly by the thought that he has no way of ensuring that the girl he'd kissed would be in bomb range when he explodes himself and of course, it hardly matters anyhow. She'd be scarred for life one way or another if she made it through alive.

The sister of the girl who had fainted, the one who had babbled at Noah in the run-up to the kiss, runs towards her fallen sibling as if Noah had stabbed her sis in the belly with a sword. There is clear accusation in her eyes as she flashes them up at Noah. The look is brief, however, and soon she's concentrating her full energy on reviving her sister.

'Oh, Gemma, oh my God, speak to me! Speak to me! You have to wake up, baby!'

Gemma then awakens, blinking her eyes several times in quick succession. Gemma's sister then looks up at Noah again, this time with a strange look, one that is a mixture of fear and loathing as well as the respect and love she still has for the pop star; all in all, a very confused stare.

'I'll leave you two girls to recover yourselves,' Noah says before turning around and walking away from the whole scene. Now back in the green room with the door shut behind him, alone once again, Noah suddenly realizes how close he had come to walking on stage with the intent of ending his life without having kept the promise he'd made to himself back at the hotel room to have one last toss before greeting the Grim Reaper. Noah is relieved beyond belief to have not only recalled this vow, but to be in a position to fulfil it as well. He begins to flick through the books he had inherited from Smiley and then thrown around the room, hoping to find something worthy of be used as masturbation fodder. He laughs as one of the first books he sees as he scans the room for material is the Koran. Noah then feels a twinge of sadness as this brings to mind the meeting with Mr Elahi of a few hours previous. Poor Mr Elahi, coming all the way to New York to see him on his pleading, only to be met with a hungover, goofy mess. Noah looks again at the copy of the Koran he'd forgotten he'd inherited, then thinks again about the visit of his former imam; he wonders if this whole series of random events might lead to Islam being blamed for what he was about to do. *Don't be stupid. No one is going to think that.* Particularly after he'd essentially laid a trail to Smiley's door. But the idea of all the hacks having to speculate about the Koran does make Noah smile once again. He places it neatly between the Bible and *Mein Kampf.*

He then quickly scouts through the rest of the reading material. Nothing that will help him fulfil his penultimate duty is in the stack as it happens. One hell of an oversight by John K, albeit a wholly unsurprising one.

In lieu of anything useful emerging from the armful of books he had immediately available, Noah attempts to recall images from *Office Sluts*. As he does so, he pulls his underpants and trousers down and grabs his limpid member, being extra careful not to knock the bomb attached to his chest in any way. He then begins to attempt to yank it to attention as his mind reels, trying desperately to picture the woman who played the secretary. The only woman's face he can conjure up, however, is Eva. Things are getting worse, not better; his penis is practically sucking itself up into Noah's body now. *Eva! That's it! I'll call her and her voice will get me there!* It's such an obvious move, Noah chastises himself for not having thought of it immediately upon deciding to pursue this exercise as he retrieves his phone from the trouser pocket that currently sits round his ankles. As he reaches down, he comes terrifyingly close to brushing the red button at his side. He breathes a sigh of relief at having luckily avoided doing so.

He finds Eva in his recent calls and presses the button to dial her with one hand while grabbing his dick with the other. He gets a brief reprieve as he anticipates his neo-Nazi former girlfriend's luscious tones. This is extremely short-lived however, as it soon dawns on him, as it rings and rings and rings, that voicemail is looking more and more likely. *No matter. I can beat off to her message.* But the disappointment hits rock bottom as another woman's voice said:

'*Welcome to the Telelux automated voice messaging service. If you would like to leave a message, speak after the tone . . .*'

This is the final blow. Noah sadly – and carefully – pulls his undergarments followed by his trousers back up, making him fully clothed again. *Nothing short of the porn actress from 'Office Sluts' suddenly knocking on my dressing-room door is going to reverse this setback.* His heart races as in the next moment, his phone rings. He desperately scrambles to answer it. Noah is so sure that it must be Eva calling him back, he doesn't even bother to look at the display.

'Hey,' he says breathlessly.

'Hi.'

His heart sinks. It's Cheryl, not Eva.

'What do you want?'

Noah says this sharply and aggressively. He doesn't mean for this to be the case, but his disappointment in it not being Eva on the other end of the line is simply too great to conceal. Cheryl breaks down into sobs. Noah takes a moment to think about what to do next.

He had had no intention of ever speaking to Cheryl again. But now that she has called him and he has answered in an ungracious tone, a rhetorical moral question is now a live one: does he try telling her again what he's about to do, or does he not? Noah quickly weighs up the pros and cons of each approach. If he tells her about the impending bombing of which he intends to be the perpetrator, she may tell someone who will listen and thus stop it from happening. Particularly now that he has the device strapped to himself; it would be a simple matter of someone searching him. Would telling Cheryl give her any peace of mind in a few hours' time? *No, it wouldn't. Actually, it would probably make things worse.* Noah attempts to come up with solid downsides to not telling Cheryl and comes up blank. Decision made.

'I'm about to go on stage, so I can't really talk right now. I'll call after the show, promise.'

He feels instantly bad for making this pledge, but too late now.

'You promise promise?' she asks.

'Unless something unforeseeably tragic happens, I'll call you,' Noah says, covering his bases.

'Okay. Noah?'

'Yes?'

'I still love you.'

Noah hadn't heard Cheryl use the 'L' word in some time and it pierces his heart a little.

'I love you too.'

He hangs up after saying this, not wanting to stretch the conversation out any further. He was lying when he told Cheryl that he loved her, but figured it was best to leave the poor girl with something, a tiny morsel of comfort after what was coming her way. A knock comes to his door. It's Jules. His phone begins to ring again. It's Cheryl, of course, more confused than ever after Noah's last words to her before hanging up. Noah ignores the call, leaving the phone ringing away on the couch as he gets up to go.

'We're on, boss,' Jules shouts through the door.

As Noah steps onto the Madison Square Garden stage, he is disappointed to feel precisely the same as he always does when he performs this ritual, wherever he might be. It's the same rush he experienced the first time he entered stage right to confront a seething mass of adoring fans, only diminished slightly from each time to the next, so that by now it was a mere flicker of the original, the change each night only noticeable across a long stretch of time, like the way your face looks the same every day even though small changes over each twenty-four-hour timespan add up to you looking geriatric one day. Noah had been hoping for a greater rush under the circumstances, a return to the full-on hit of the old days, but to no avail. It feels like the same old day job, even with the stakes this high. He smiles at the fans, as always, same old grin. They notice nothing in the fact that he is a touch more reticent than normal. *I suppose I've been a bit shit for a while now. Like Elvis when he was losing it, steadily over time. It's so gradual none of the fans really noticed until it got way out of control and Elvis was falling asleep on stage.* He thinks about Elvis a little more and then a thought occurs to him that makes him laugh, one about Elvis and a toilet. The spontaneous joy that splashes across the singer's face instantly translates to the crowd, who proceed to go wild with excitement. They clearly think the giggle was for them. *At least I won't die like Elvis did, fallen off the john, leaving a shit behind him. I'm going out in a blaze of glory instead.* It isn't the

179

thought of the Elvis bathroom scene that causes the smile so much as the thought of what he is about to do, the perversity of it. Although Noah has decided that his need to make John K. Smiley suffer is the principle reason for the crime he's about to perpetrate, at least a minor part of it is also the sheer *outré* sense of it all; the *épater le bourgeois* involved that completely goes against the grain of his entire singing career. He is about to do the opposite of what is expected of him for the first time in a long time. This thought frees Noah up to enjoy the spectacle and all nervousness and second thoughts melt away, aided more than he would ever admit to himself by the crowd's reaction to his laugh.

Noah launches into his usual opening number, the song that was his first hit, 'Baby You're Something Special to Me'. He had always hated it, right from the moment it was first shown to him on acetate.

In the weeks between him having heard the song that would turn him into an international signing sensation and having to record the thing, Noah spent a lot of time regretting having signed to the label in the first place. The company had been so eager to get him on their roster; perhaps he should have held out for more control. As it stood, he was essentially a stooge. The bigwigs told him that while he could technically veto the song they chose for him to be his first hit, it was rather unsubtly communicated at the same time that this would be an unwise course of action for reasons he'd have to dare to find out for himself should he actually take this regrettable option up.

He heard the acetate a couple of weeks after he'd signed the recording contract. Murray had asked Noah to come to the record company's head offices for a meeting. He wasn't told beforehand what it was going to be about. When he walked in and all of the execs were gathered around the table, Noah smelled the worst. He actually thought for a moment that they were going to kick him off the label, before he'd even recorded anything, but quickly realized they wouldn't do it that way if that's what they were intending. He'd simply have gotten a form letter via his lawyer or Murray.

'Have a seat, Noah,' the president of the company said to him. They had never previously met. Another man ran into the room holding a record, an actual old-time record, sweating nervously. He was short and fat and out of breath. He placed the record on a turntable that was sitting against the far wall, then kneeled down and picked up the needle and held it above the now spinning platter, like an executioner holding the axe above a condemned man's head. He was clearly waiting for a signal from someone.

'Noah, listen carefully to what you're about to hear,' said another suit he'd never met. He had no idea who this one was and never found out. 'It's your future.'

The president pointed then at the little corpulent man in the corner, who proceeded to put the needle carefully down upon the vinyl. In the following moment, an extra-cheesy dance version of 'Baby You're Something Special to Me' erupted from four speakers, one for each corner of the room. It was sung by a generic wannabe, someone who clearly wanted to be a pop star, probably thought that singing on the acetate was his big break, not knowing that he'd already been placed in a category from which becoming a pop star was an impossibility. Noah was instantly repulsed. He also knew that the nameless man in the suit was correct: he was listening to his future. That without a doubt he would sing this terrible song and it would in turn be a massive hit that would launch his singing career.

He spent most of the following night tossing and turning, tempted at one point to call Murray, right then and there at three twenty-three in the morning and tell him that he wasn't going to do it; that this wasn't what he'd gone into music to achieve and that they would have to find another song, something that suited him better, no matter what the suits thought or said. But Noah chickened out of such a bold move and found himself in the studio, eight a.m., as tired as he would ever feel in his life, having to try and add life to the horrible, wretched song that he knew he'd be singing for the rest of his days. *Baby, you're something special to me. To my heart you're the one with the key. Stay by my side and then you'll see. That baby, you're something special to me.* As he began to sing the chorus for the first time, which opens the song à la 'She Loves You' (pointed out by Murray immediately following that first hearing in the room with the suits, a comment which made Noah almost vomit then and there in the record label's lobby), the pop star did what would soon come naturally: he closed his mind down, taking himself to a cosy place, filled with things only he liked and people who only liked him. It was remarkably similar to the place he would transport himself to when he was being beaten up by his father during his childhood.

In the middle of singing his first hit for the five millionth (*but very last!*) time to the throngs of screaming kids packed into Madison Square Garden, Noah notices Murray giving him a thumbs up from backstage. Noah makes note of the fact that it's the first time he's seen his manager all day long. Given he'd set out to intentionally avoid him, Noah celebrates this little moral victory with another smile that makes all the kiddies in the front few rows, the rows that were about to be directly affected by the bomb that was strapped to their hero's chest – unbeknownst to them, of course – scream in ecstasy.

The best thing about being a world-famous pop star on stage in front of thousands of adoring fans is its exclusivity; there are less than a thousand people who have ever lived, in the history of the human race, who have ever experienced this sort of adoration and know what it feels like. Even with a bomb strapped to his chest, Noah still finds himself loving the whole charade as much as he ever did.

Oddly enough, he hadn't planned exactly when during the concert itself he would bring the whole thing to an unexpected and abrupt end. He had thought that perhaps he should wait until he was well into the concert before doing it, perhaps even finish the whole thing and do it as an encore. *The people should get value for their money after all.* But as he approaches the completion of his first number, Noah suddenly has a change of heart and thinks seriously about pressing the button during the closing bars of 'Baby You're Something Special to Me' itself. He thinks again and decides not to. No, he would take everyone out with at least two songs. It then occurs to him what song he should sing next.

'Hey guys, do you remember how to play "The World's a Stranger to Me"?' Noah says into the mic so that the whole crowd could hear. It is actually a question directed at the band. The professional musicians who make up Noah's backing group instinctively all look to their right as Noah asks this, towards the disapproving face of Murray. The manager shakes his head definitively. The band obviously thinks this will be the end of the matter, but little do they know that tonight's a special night.

'Oh dear. I had a whole new song I wrote that I wanted to sing for you guys here tonight but my manager, Murray, has decided against it. What do you guys have to say to Murray about that?'

Thinking this is a piece of pantomime, the crowd mock boos Noah's manager. Most of the crowd will not be aware of who Murray is or what function he performs, of course, not even the real hardcore fans. Some managers, your Colonel Tom Parker types, are famous in their own right. Murray is much more of a lurking in the shadows type of manager who is completely uninterested in the spotlight. He glowers in a paternal sort of way at his client, shaking his head once more. Noah looks at him and then slowly raises his hand and gives Murray the finger. He does this openly and in full view of the crowd, who are confused but cheer along anyhow. Murray then realizes something is up with his client. Probably drinking again, Murray thinks to himself. The long-suffering manager waves his hands despondently towards the stage, giving in.

'Right, guys, it looks like you all changed Murray's mind. This next song is one we left off the last album, and tonight is the only night on the tour I'm going to sing it.'

Having been informed of the fact that they were about to witness 'Noahistory', the crowd goes even crazier than they had been up until that point. The band, meanwhile, has an impromptu huddle, talking over what each of them remembers about this tune they had only played a couple of times and at that not for several months. Satisfied that they can pull it off, and having their professional pride piqued by this sudden, unforeseen challenge, the band leader smiles and gives a thumbs up to Noah. Seconds later, the song begins. Noah feels a tingle all over his body that he hadn't been expecting when he made the snap decision to sing this particular number. It had been a huge point of contention between Noah and Murray when choosing the final tracks for the last album (*it really will be the last album!*). Noah had written the song himself and felt proud of it, while Murray thought it jarred with the rest of the album as it was far too dark, both musically and lyrically. Murray did have a point, but Noah felt he'd earned a moment of truth; a single song in which he could be allowed to express himself the way he would ideally like to. Murray saw that letting Noah have one song would lead to a demand for more, the old give them an inch and they'll take a mile theory; as a result, he was immovable in his demand that the song not make the final cut. In the end, Noah had to concede his will to that of the boss, as always, as had happened ever since they had first met.

How Murray had become Noah's manager in the first place was rather strange. They were introduced through Smiley – although John K. didn't seem to know Murray all that well at the time. Noah didn't like Murray when they first met; the pop manager spent a great deal of the initial meeting talking about horse racing, which is something he always does with everyone but was a move which alienated Noah greatly as he associated horse racing with his father's unfortunate gambling habit. The proto-pop star felt that the prospective

184

manager brought little to the table. He had dealt with a few minor acts and been around a while, but none of his clients had ever gone big. But as always, Smiley talked him round. Noah always did whatever those around him told him to do; back in the early days but also ever since. He has always been scared of making a decision that might turn out to be wrong; one that would cost him his stardom. If it's someone else's call that leads to his downfall, he could somehow live with that. This is what makes the decision he made on the aeroplane the previous day so singular. It may in fact be the one major career decision he'd made without consultation. Except, even that's not true, when Noah has to think about it. Smiley was heavily involved, as per usual.

As 'The World's a Stranger to Me' reaches its chorus at Madison Square Garden, Noah feels a tingle go down his spine and feels alive in a way he hadn't in a long time. He tries to figure out if it's the rebellious act of singing the song Murray wanted locked away for ever to a packed crowd – or if it's the fact that he is mere minutes away from committing suicide/mass murder. It doesn't particularly matter to Noah, when he considers it. In some ways, the invidious act he is about to carry out is a way of getting back at Murray as well as Smiley, and indeed all of those record company bigwigs; everyone who had told him what to do over the past several years. Noah suddenly hopes, in a way that makes his heart swell, that Murray will be killed in the explosion too.

The song reaches its middle section: a reasonably long, at least by the standards of anodyne pop music, instrumental bit that leaves Noah to revel in his thoughts, the final thoughts he figures he is ever going to think. He considers then the finality of the act he is about to commit, not only for him but for all those he is about to take along with him unwillingly and unknowingly. He feels surer than ever that there is no god whatsoever, and more to the point no real purpose to the universe either. *All is random and meaningless nonsense. But if that's the case why end things like this? If this is about eternal fame, then surely if everything is meaningless, fame is meaningless too.* Noah gets hung up on this one. Somehow, even though all of his existential reasoning leads to the conclusion that fame must be meaningless, it still, somehow, has meaning to Noah. The meaning of fame never dissipates for him. It's like a magic trick you can never work out the method to. Noah tries again, digging deep into his soul to try and accept the notion that fame is without any true value. He realizes as he performs this exercise that it could be the difference between life and death; if he can debunk fame, then what he is about to do cannot possibly be justified.

Then in a flash, it comes to him: he sees through fame, just like that, as he could see through everything else. Sort of like the moment when you die, Noah sees his whole career go flashing before his eyes. And like instant psychotherapy, he sees it all for what it has been: a virtually pointless exercise that only had one positive: it had left him financially independent. He then focuses on his wealth. Although his money didn't have meaning in any larger existential sense, in other words beyond his own fleeting existence or anything else for that matter, he saw now that he could at last solve his previous conundrum, the one that had at least partially led him to this plan to take his own life and the lives of however many fans stood in bomb range. Seeing that fame was meaningless meant he could finally live without it. Which meant he could quit the whole game, never seeing the likes of Murray or Jules or people like Gemma ever again. He could simply take his money and live out his life on an island somewhere, in peace. As for his other motivation for the intended bombing, the ruining of John K. Smiley's life, Noah works out instantly that there will be multiple opportunities on that front in the months ahead that don't involve blowing himself into a million tiny pieces.

So that's that, he decides: *I'm not going to do it after all.* He won't press that button, hung so delicately inside the cuff of his jacket, looking to all the world like a wayward fashion statement. He'll sing out this concert and then announce his retirement from the pop game as soon as humanly possible. Noah smiles as he thinks about Murray's face upon hearing the words come out of Noah's mouth; the absolute horror as his manager realizes the gravy train has come to an abrupt halt. *Yes, this is going to be an even sweeter revenge on all those fuckers, me bowing out randomly. Perhaps I should do it tonight. Perhaps I should do it right after this song is finished.*

But then, Noah sees a kid in the front row with a T-shirt with a slogan emblazoned across it that reads: 'NOAH HASTINGS SUCKS BALLS'. As Noah reads the shirt, the kid wearing it understands implicitly that his greatest wish in the world has come true and with that, his face erupts into a world record smile. He raises his right hand and extends his middle finger towards the pop idol, while mouthing the words 'Fuck you, Hastings'. And it is this that puts Noah back on course. *That little shit is going to be made to pay. You think you're getting the last laugh now, asshole, but you wait. Not long now.* He feels for the button in his sleeve and feeling it there makes Noah more determined than ever to go through with the plan he had hatched on the plane the previous day. This is because seeing that kid proves to Noah that although he could convince himself that fame was meaningless for a few seconds, all it took to remind him of the fact that this was a lie was a stupid kid in a stupid T-shirt mouthing some stupid words in his direction. *It's destiny. Seeing that kid was one in a thousand but see him I did. Tonight's the night after all.*

As 'The World's a Stranger to Me' comes to an end, the band all look towards Noah for a sign of what to do next. He mouths the title of the next song, 'Love You Like Never Before', in their direction and they duly respond. It is one of Noah's bigger hits and the crowd erupts with joy once again. Noah looks at the kid with the middle finger and the T-shirt. The little prick cannot believe his luck and is about to offer his finger towards the stage once again when Noah turns away from him and begins to sing the opening verse. *This is the song. The last song. Ever.* This thought makes Noah put a little more oomph into his performance than usual and this in turn makes the crowd go even more wild. Girls begin to whisper amongst each other – are they witness to a Noah comeback of sorts? A new song out of the blue and a fresh oomph? The pop star responds to these unheard but entirely felt rumours (Noah is in touch with his fans, after all) by dancing his ass off, whirling like he hadn't done since he had first made it. He can feel the crowd rising, getting excited.

He keeps singing and dancing, singing and dancing. During the instrumental break, he surveys the audience, hoping to catch a glimpse of someone he knows. No dice; simply the usual sea of unknown but happy faces, bobbing along to the terrible music. In the midst of this, Noah is struck by another ping of doubt all of a sudden. Again, it seems ridiculous that he is about to blow himself up in front of an audience. Why? Why not? He'd been suicidal for a long time and if you're going to go out, go out with a bang – literally so. He can't go on the way things are, but as Andy with the beers on the plane and the kid with the finger in the front row both demonstrated aptly, he can't go on without the adoration either. Fame – can't live with it, can't live without it. Despite all of this, Noah also can't work up the courage to do it yet. He sings the final verse and chorus of 'Love You Like Never Before' and soaks in the applause afterwards. The band looks to him to see what comes next. Noah motions to them to hang loose for the moment.

'I want to tell you all tonight that times have been tough for me lately.'

The comment comes off as weird – something is up with Noah and every fan can feel it suddenly. An eerie silence descends. Pop music, like any other creative form, has strict rules of engagement. Stepping outside of them, truly stepping outside of them as Noah is doing now, creates instant tension.

Noah continues speaking into the microphone.

'It's weird how you can have all these fans but feel totally alone sometimes. You know, I have a confession to make . . .'

Noah pauses for a moment, unsure himself of what he's going to say next.

'. . . I really like hotel porn.'

A few of the kids start laughing, as you'd expect after the last comment, but more than a few others start crying. The whole atmosphere is now surreal beyond description. Noah realizes he's ended up in exactly the position he had promised internally he wouldn't put himself in when he came up with his plan aboard the plane yesterday. The whole bombing was supposed to be nice and smooth, no wrinkles in the system, everyone boogieing until the final chord, all leading up to that moment that only Noah will have known was coming and that he would not have presaged in the slightest. Now here he was, admitting to his porn preferences in front of Madison Square Garden.

Realizing there was nothing to do but keep the show going, Noah motions to the band to play the next scheduled song, which happens to be 'I'm Going to Dance Until Late, Late, Late'. The band do as they are instructed, and most of the crowd tries to forget about the bizarre revelation Noah had laid on them and enjoy themselves again. Noah goes to sing the first line and finds that he can't remember any of the words. He decides that this matters less than getting something out of his larynx, so he goes to sing whatever comes to mind first. But he then realizes nothing is coming out; he's suddenly lost his voice. What's all the worse for Noah is that this is an almost exact replica of a nightmare he'd had repeatedly since he had first achieved stardom – being on stage in front of thousands and losing his voice out of the blue. He tries to force something to come out, anything, but nothing comes.

Noah has an emotional breakdown. He begins to cry openly, unreservedly. The band members all turn to look towards Murray, silently asking him what they should do: keep playing through this or stop? Murray frantically waves them on, figuring that having the band cut out would be worse than hoping Noah gets his shit together out there and pulls through.

Noah realizes two things that fill him with an indescribable horror: one, he'll never sing another note ever again, and two, he is going to die in a matter of seconds. Noah feels for the button. Having got a firm hold on it, he closes his eyes and firmly presses his thumb down.

An article by Philip A. Simmonds published in the
New York Express*, promoting his book, *The Trial
***of the Century: John K. Smiley and America*,**
December 3rd, 2025

It is difficult writing about a lost cause; something you think everyone should care about as much as you still do. Since America
discovered that John K. Smiley, a Christian preacher, was the one
behind the Hastings bombing, and not some imagined Muslim
monster, the incident and its complicated aftermath has become of
ever-diminishing interest to the public. I am fighting against the
grain with my book, but I shan't give in. I think what happened to
Smiley after his incarceration is vital to understanding America in
the 2020s.

Let me take you back four years to when Smiley was first arrested
for his part in the bombing that took place on June 16th, 2021, one
that resulted in the deaths of 92 people, including Noah Hastings.
At the time, the name John K. Smiley alone struck fear into almost
everyone in America. Perhaps it was simply the knowledge of what
he had done that created this impression in people. It is still hard to
imagine the man as a preacher, even after all of the time I've spent
with him. Having people look up to him as he stands at the pulpit,
listening to him as a sane, never mind sagacious voice is impossible
to envision. He looked to most people back in 2022 like the face of
evil, a sort of death's head incarnate. Having interviewed him on so
many different occasions I ended up literally losing count – just
keeping track of and filing the Smiley interviews became a genuine
problem for me at one stage – I can also say that what comes out of

his mouth about ninety-five per cent of the time reinforces this visual impression, albeit in a round-about sort of fashion I hope to be able to explain during the course of this article.

I will never forget my experience of sitting in the press gallery of the US Supreme Court, having yet to meet the man, and seeing John K. Smiley walk in every day. The look of defiance, of 'I do not recognize this court' spread across his face, was solid and consistent, never faltering for even a moment. Smiley always seemed completely convinced of himself – upon entry, when sitting in the dock and particularly when on the witness stand. That's before I get to the almost poetic interchanges with the representative for the prosecution that one waited for amongst all of the more run-of-the-mill technical witness statements about explosive devices and their use; the back and forths that despite seeming to cement Smiley's guilt in the matter, never appeared to wear down his resolve that he was in the right. In all my years of covering legal proceedings, I have never seen anything like it. I will highlight only the most relevant moment from my tapes of the trial:

PROSECUTION: Mr Samson, you admit to trying to coax Mr Hastings into committing terrorist atrocities at many points across several years?

SMILEY: To state for the record once more, I would prefer to be called Mr Smiley. I admit only to trying to convince Noah to see the Lord like I do. To see that sometimes the Lord demands a little something extra.

PROSECUTION: Please answer the question, Mr Samson . . .

SMILEY: That's Mr Smiley, if you don't mind, sir.

PROSECUTION: The question, Mr Samson, was again: did you attempt to convince Mr Hastings to commit terrorist acts, such as the one he finally committed on June sixteenth, 2021, repeatedly across the course of several years?

SMILEY: I tried to steer Noah in the right direction. But I failed, your honour (*note: directly addressing the judge at this point, as he so often did*). He went to that dang mosque every day for months, he boozed it up on and off for years, he fucked that Austrian whore, that Nazi bitch . . .

Smiley was at this point asked to watch his language by the judge, a request that had to be made repeatedly to Smiley throughout the trial.

PROSECUTION: Is the answer yes or no, Mr Samson?
SMILEY: That's Mr Smiley, son.
PROSECUTION: Yes or no?
SMILEY: The answer is whatever you'd like it to be.

This form of baiting the prosecution went on incessantly throughout the trial. Some days, Smiley had to be stopped by the judge while in the middle of what seemed like a madness-inspired homily about the evils of Islam and the need for our young to be ready for the challenge faced by 'the enrolment of foreign religions' (Smiley is particularly given to malapropisms – I think he meant 'encroachment' in that instance), only to once again become completely calm, apologize to the judge, right as the threat of being hauled out of court for contempt seemed about to be carried out.

The trial was long and tiresome as a result. The reason I believe that I have ultimately ended up being the one writing a book about Smiley, the trial and what it says about American society, as opposed to someone else I mean, is that I was one of the few people who could stick out coming to that courtroom day after day after gruelling day. Many fell by the wayside throughout its duration, simply unable to take another day of Smiley's rants, his misused words, his bitter hatred of everything he fails to understand (i.e. most things in the world). The other journalists also sensed something I didn't: that the story was of increasingly faltering interest to most Americans.

I must confess that it was not my ability to endure that was my advantage. I'm slightly ashamed to admit that I had become simply too addicted to the Smiley character (for he is simply a character created by Jeremiah Samson after all) to give in to my own sense of the story being a lost cause. I stayed to see him being found guilty of every crime he was accused of; I was there when Jeremiah George Samson, known to himself and his associates as John K. Smiley, was sentenced to death by lethal injection.

Despite the long hours spent in the courtroom, it was after the sentence had been passed that my real work began. For it was then – after a difficult but thankfully brief set of negotiations between my agent and Smiley himself – that I started to regularly interview the subject of what was to become my book.

Smiley was, predictably in retrospect, a hard person to get under the skin of. My first three interviews yielded little of substance as he tended to offer terse, uninformative and wholly unusable answers to the questions I threw at him. It's fair to say that during this spell I seriously wondered whether I'd ever get Smiley to loosen up around me, and if this wasn't possible what sort of book I'd be able to write at the end of it all. I contemplated giving up on the whole project a couple of times. What I did instead of surrendering was to collect secondary data. After all, even if Smiley wasn't being forthcoming himself, I was still getting access every couple of days to what was a unique world.

It can come as little surprise that John K. Smiley had a rather large fan club during his stay on death row in Arlington, Virginia, one that grew steadily as the weeks and months wore on, as his death at the hands of the state grew theoretically closer. The fans mostly came from the same neck of the woods as Smiley himself: the forgotten towns of the American South. They would write him words of encouragement, as if Smiley were a freedom fighter on the frontlines of some war in the Third World, battling for the good guys. What came as the biggest surprise to me when reading these letters – which, surprisingly, Smiley was willing to let me do, even during these tense opening moments of our relationship, when he clearly did not trust me even slightly – was the level of articulation many of them possessed. I will give you only some of the more note-worthy additions here:

'The aggressive secularization of our society is only stopped through the vision of people such as yourself, Reverend Smiley. God bless you.'

'Christians throughout the United States need to understand the enemy we face in Islam. They also need to realize that many of us will need to die in the inevitable battle. If my child had been one of those kids at Madison Square Garden on that fateful night, I would gladly have sacrificed his life for the betterment of our nation.'

'I thank God every day for you, John Smiley. Finally, someone who is willing to sacrifice his own freedom, his own life even, for the advancement of the Christian faith. Jesus will give you your reward when you meet him shortly.'

It was through these letters, and my constant questions about them, that I finally got through to John K. Smiley. As we discussed their contents, the preacher-cum-holy war terrorist finally opened up to me.

'This one's great,' he said to me one day, flashing a smile I had yet to even get a hint of previously. 'Sent me a picture of her bare ass. Jesus, I love the fans.'

When showing me a letter which contained this sort of thing, nudity, or something that was of a similarly lewd nature, Smiley would always feel the need to 'get serious' with me again immedi-ately after putting the profane on display.

'But most of the letters I receive are from upstanding, God-fearing folks, you understand? I get letters from all across the world, every day, from people who can see that my crusade is a righteous one.'

I felt tempted to point out to him on many occasions that the 'all across the world' demarcation regarding where his correspondence was coming from seemed to mostly consist of Louisiana, Mississippi and Alabama. However, it had taken a lot to build up my goodwill with him, and I wasn't about to fritter it away on pointless details.

'That whole thing at Madison Square Garden, yep, I masterminded it,' Smiley said completely unprompted by me one day, this shortly after my initial breakthrough with him.

'What I want to know is this: how did you convince Noah Hastings to participate?' I asked him in return. I'll never forget the way that Smiley grimaced at me, revealing his fierce, vicious side in a way that he'd never let slip with me previously (and never subsequently did again). As usual when you are dealing with a sociopath like John K. Smiley, the glance he allowed me at his feral side disappeared almost as quickly as it had surfaced. With his usual bland, man-of-the-people face restored, Smiley told me:

'Noah was always – always – secretly at least, a true believer. Someone who was willing to do whatever it took for the Christian faith to flourish. Now, I know what you're going to say: what about the booze, and the Nazis, and the Muslim crap then, huh?'

He made a hand gesture that struck me at the time as slightly camp. I had no idea what it was meant to signify and was about to ask him about it when he continued.

'Those were all simply divergents (note: I think he meant "diversions" here). Hell, we all get diverged sometimes. But the Almighty, he brings us back to where we need to be. That's what he did with Noah – just when we needed him to be in the right place at the right time. With the right weapon. That's where I come in, of course.'

At this point he laughed; the sort of expression of emotion you only get from sociopaths, with their strange, disconnected sense of humour that always tends to involve other people's misfortune and/or misery. Remaining untaken by Smiley's 'wit', I asked him if he had any regrets about what had happened; if he ever felt guilty for the ninety-two people who were killed in the blast, including Hastings himself, particularly given Smiley's story is that it was he who talked the singer into the whole thing. The preacher shook his head, not an ounce of sympathy behind his cold, dead, shark-like eyes.

'Those people needed to be saved and Noah and I helped save them. Better that they are in heaven now, cleansed, than had they gone on living their sinful lives and then been damned for all eternity.'

I asked Smiley about his childhood, about his time as a Baptist preacher, and about how he eventually became embroiled in legal troubles around the fraudulent behaviour for which he was eventually convicted in Louisiana. I ask him to tell me what he can about meeting Abraham Hastings in prison and how they became good friends. His tales were often long, difficult to follow and ultimately contradictory; sometimes in conflict with each other, but sometimes even within themselves. Once he told me the story of how he invented the name, John K. Smiley. He said it came to him in a dream, one he attributed to divine intervention. But later in the same story, which by that point had gone on a sideways diversion involving Abraham Hastings and a drinking game they used to play which required a pack of cards, a bottle of Sambuca, and a fish that had gone slightly off, Smiley mentioned that Abraham Hastings had actually thought up the Smiley sobriquet, having seen a character by that name on a cartoon he had caught while looking after Noah when he was a toddler.

I quickly got the sense that Smiley was always making most of what he was telling me up as he went along. He struck me as a man with a past he largely regretted, one which had ended up taking him far from the principles he had joined the church to espouse. It became clear from our conversations that he viewed his acts concerning the events of June 16th to be an attempt at redemption on his part. I asked him about this directly during one of my last sessions with him. His reply was striking.

'I suppose I did some things in my past I wish I hadn't of done. Do I see the New York thing as a sort of, making up for past sins type of thing? Maybe in a way. We're all sinners after all, and I like I said, my past is not free from fault. I'd like to think, though, that even if my past had been perfect, I would have done what I did anyhow when the time was right. That I would have asked Noah to make the sacrifice that he made regardless of any personal motivations.'

I will add at this point that the interviews I conducted with Smiley are among the most affecting in which I have ever been involved, from a purely personal perspective anyhow. I went into this project an agnostic; one who might go to church on Christmas Day if it was close to home and I was with family members who were keen to attend. I am now, directly as a result of my exposure to Smiley on death row in Virginia, a confirmed atheist, someone who wants nothing whatsoever to do with Christianity ever again. Some people find it easy to divorce this horrible man from his faith; to say that every bowl has a bad nut or two, so don't condemn the whole batch. The problem for me is that Smiley's psychopathology shines a perfect light on all of monotheism's problems in a way that I find inescapable. His absolute confidence that the murder of almost a hundred people was the right thing to do, with the inability for logical realizations to occur as a result of imbedded religious faith, demonstrates such faith as irredeemable to me. The idea that sacrifice of independent thought prevented one from being able to shake themselves out of possibly doing something irreparable, unforgiveable, murderous, destroyed any faith I had in the idea of faith itself – probably forever. The late, great Christopher Hitchens once said, 'In the ordinary moral universe, the good will do the best they can, the worst will do the worst they can, but if you want to make good people do wicked things, you'll need religion.'

Following my final interview with John K. Smiley, I only returned one more time to the prison in which he had become a resident. It was on the day of his execution, a long time after the last meeting I'd had with the man. Outside, there were two distinct camps gathered, the pro-Smileys and the antis. The Smiley fan club was a weird mix of old folks holding crucifixes, bikers who had come as apparently Smiley had by this point become some sort of outlaw hero amongst a certain set, anti-death penalty activists who were only there because they come to every execution to protest and finally, a few doe-eyed Christian activist types who looked a bit freaked out by it all. This group was far more vocal and boisterous than the anti-Smiley bunch, most of whom it turned out had some connection to one of the victims of the Madison Square Garden bombing and had shown up hoping for some closure to their grief. I only stayed outside briefly as I was going to have the privilege of being in the room when Smiley died; I had requested this of the state, who had kindly accepted and given me a 'VIP' ringside seat. I was out there long enough to witness how horribly treated the antis were by the Smiley fan club, taunted with crosses and pictures of burnt corpses, one with a caption reading 'BETTER TO DIE AND BE SAVED THAN TO PERISH A SINNER', never realizing the horrible irony of that statement in relation to June 16th, 2021, Noah Hastings and John K. Smiley.

The execution itself was simple and yet somehow difficult to describe. I found out, as I took my seat and asked a few people close by, that the reason the families of the Hastings bombing victims were outside with the throng instead of inside came down to the fact that the execution room holds a mere one hundred and fifteen people, and the requests from close relatives of the victims to attend numbered over three hundred. The state apparently then tried to prioritize who got in and who didn't, found it impossible to include some but not others and finally decided, in what must count as a strange political move on their part, to decline to offer invites to any of the victims' relatives whatsoever. Learning this made me feel incredibly guilty that I was sitting there, warm and cozy, while the people who wanted and deserved their places (as much as one can deserve a seat at an execution) were denied simply because there were too damn many of them. What made this feeling worse were the empty chairs around me, reserved by members of the national press who had failed to turn up in the end. Then I remembered I was about to see a man die in front of me and as a result, felt somewhat less fortunate about the whole thing.

When Smiley came in, the expression on his face was the one he almost always wore. Sort of blank with an air of pretension about it, with a latent smile peeking out from behind the covers. It didn't change when they strapped him to the bed. He lay there, peering out at us as we all were sitting there, watching him, as if he were an actor in a particularly bad community play we had all come to see because one of our friends was in it.

His face only changed when they inserted the cannula into his right arm; for a moment, a nanosecond maybe, a look of terror crossed his face. But like when he let his anger expose itself to me for a mere moment when I interviewed him, his composure instantly returned. As the drugs that would put him to sleep (these are administered first; then the chemicals that stop breathing; then ones that halt the heart), I swear to the god I no longer have any doubt does not exist that John K. Smiley looked right at me, me and me alone, and winked. Or perhaps I merely hallucinated that he did, I don't know. Watching a man being killed in front of you, even via a painless drug routine, is an extremely surreal experience, and as a result I don't entirely trust my own sensory recall of the event. A few seconds later, he was asleep. A few seconds after that, he was dead. It was a quick procedure.

I remember getting the hell out of there as fast as one can do from a high-security military prison facility as soon as Smiley's pulse stopped. I went to the first bar I could find, a cheap truckers'-style joint off of the I-80, where I decided to drink myself back to sanity. I was into my third scotch on the rocks when it occurred to me that I was in a state of semi-grief for John K. Smiley. I laughed, drawing some stares from the group of large men nearby who probably thought I was insane. Grieve for that murdering, psychopathic asshole? What would possess me to do that? I found this easy to answer, even sitting in that terrible bar semi-ripped on scotch: whatever else he was, he was a human being, and a human being that I had spent time with, gotten to know. I didn't miss him, or wish he were there at that moment to talk to me. I just wished that he wasn't dead.

As I finished that third drink, the one I decided would be my last in that particular establishment, I also figured out why Smiley had turned me atheist. It wasn't the fact that he'd killed people in the name of Jesus. It was that his bizarre gaggle of fans rejoiced in the deaths of the people he killed, doing so because they didn't, couldn't, see death for what it is: the end. That's why religion is so corrosive. By setting up the idea of eternal life, of life after life, it thus debases life – and by extension, death. And by extension further still, murder.

'Noah Hastings and the forgotten tragedy' by David O'Willery, article in *Persons*, June 2026 edition,

I write this on the fifth anniversary of the bombing that occurred on June 16th, 2021 at Madison Square Garden in New York City. That evening, ninety-two people died including Noah Hastings, a pop star famous the world over who had been the principle attraction of that evening's entertainment. It turned out that Hastings had the bomb strapped to his own chest – and that he himself had detonated the device.

I was at ground zero that night. While having not attended the concert itself, I was at the aftermath within the hour. The sight of paramedics heading in and out of the flaming building carrying dead bodies on stretchers is still one that haunts my dreams on occasion. Like all wretched spectacles, you had to be there in the moment to truly absorb the full horror of it all.

It is worth mentioning the details of the disaster again as a recap. For it is strange the degree to which an atrocity that loomed so large in the American consciousness for an extended period of time has now come to be semi-forgotten. The deaths of almost a hundred people can never be truly erased, of course. Yet the degree to which we turned our backs on Hastings Wednesday after the arrest of John K. Smiley is a remarkable look into the American soul and psyche.

It is also easy to misremember the degree to which the John K. Smiley theory was denigrated within the mainstream media prior to his arrest. The mention of it in major newspapers caused the downfall of several promising careers, most notably that of Nina Hargreaves, whose standing as a journalist has never recovered, sadly, in spite of being proven correct on the issue that led to her dismissal. Once the FBI had announced that Islamic fundamentalism was to blame, it was hard for anyone outside of certain minority communities to accept that such a diagnosis had proven to be a false one until it was unavoidable.

After John K. Smiley was arrested for his part in the crime, America seemed to completely lose interest in the Noah Hastings story, almost overnight. It seemed to bring the story to a satisfying end for most Americans somehow. This phenomenon says uncomfortable things about our country. We collectively frothed at the mouth when it was thought that Islamism was what was behind a bombing in the centre of New York City. Yet we felt strangely calmed when we discovered that instead it was the work of a Christian preacher, trying to build his own terrorist vision of the faith. If anything, the John K. Smiley discovery should have made us even more scared about why June 16th had happened.

I've come to the conclusion that America has a deep-seated fear of Islam that has now wound itself into the very DNA of the nation. I believe the idea that this religious faith could have infiltrated the mind of a young, homegrown, apple-pie pop star was unthinkably terrifying to the vast majority of our countrymen. If my thesis is correct, the fear that rose in the wake of the Hastings' bombing had nothing to do with the number of dead, or the fact that a beloved star had turned out to be a suicidal murderer. It was simply that he had supposedly fallen for Mohammed's teachings that was the problem.

After the Smiley arrest, the Left felt vindicated by the idea that Christians could be murderers (their own form of cultural relativism at work there), while at the same time feeling relieved Islam wasn't involved, which meant they did not need to do any soul-searching themselves about their attitudes towards Palestine, or their inbuilt favouritism towards Muslims (over Jews and Christians in particular). The Right felt good about the fact that Islam hadn't gotten as far into the American mindset as they had feared, all while comfortably accepting that the doctrines of the Christian Right will always produce a few murderous weirdos of the Timothy McVeigh variety, ones who can be dismissed as irrelevant.

Perhaps I am alone in feeling scared about what Hastings Wednesday being left behind and forgotten means for America. Perhaps it is long overdue for me to join the crowd and forget about it all as well. But I can't. I think we missed the chance to learn some big lessons five years ago and I fear we will never get another chance to learn them ever again.

'As the war in the Middle East goes on and on, the region discovers a new hero', by James Adams, foreign correspondent for the *New York Sentinel*, June 16th, 2026

With America's re-introduction of conscription for the first time since the Vietnam War now four months old, the conflict in the Middle East has all the makings of a world war. The Russians, the Chinese, even the Europeans in their usual forgettable, tokenistic way are involved and getting in deeper with every week that passes.

Five years ago today, a young pop star named Noah Hastings strapped an incredibly powerful bomb to his chest and killed himself and almost a hundred of his fans. The aftermath rocked America for a little over a year, with seemingly little else talked about in the media.

'If a pop star did that with the new generation of personal bombs floating around the Middle East, he could take out the lower portion of Manhattan with it,' said Bashir Dinladi, my Farsi and Turkish translator. Everyone's an expert on explosives in the Middle East these days.

Noah Hastings has been all but forgotten about in the last three years. In America, at least. Here in Cairo and in other parts of the Arabic world, the Hastings story has taken on what can only be described as mystical proportions. As a news story, the John K. Smiley one was hundreds of times bigger than the original Hastings bombing break in Cairo, Baghdad, Tehran and Beirut. The original story was about how Islam had been blamed for something in America, which hardly stirs the pulse in this part of the world anymore. The Smiley story was the opposite. Islam had been demonized and then it turned out there was a Christian preacher behind the crime. It could only have been worse if Smiley had been a rabbi.

John K. Smiley has even become a sort of bizarrely revered cult figure throughout the Middle East (and indeed throughout most of the developing world), his face taking its place on T-shirts sold in Amman souks beside old stalwarts like Che Guevara and Bob Marley. This seems counter-intuitive at first glance to a western observer. Shouldn't Smiley have been taken as part of the American plot against Islam, this Christian preacher who said he did what he did as a way of asserting Christianity's deserved dominance over Islam? All of that is ignored in favour of the notion that he was someone who stood up to the American system – and the American system turned around and killed him. He has been taken on board as another martyr in the ongoing jihad against the United States of America.

With Smiley the centre of the story for Arabs, they take his character and then change the events to suit their anti-American viewpoint. Hastings wanted to become a Muslim. The American government found out and then assassinated him. They then blamed it on Islam, sparking mass Islamophobia throughout the country, which was a large part of the original intent of the entire exercise. Then a man named John K. Smiley was going to speak up about the truth of what actually happened when the American government had him put to death to keep him quiet. There are variants to this basic outline but this is the essential shape of how the John K. Smiley story is understood to have taken place from Tangiers to Islamabad.

Anti-American feeling in the Middle East, and indeed the entire Muslim world, has hardened into a passionate hatred throughout most of the population that dwarves even the level of feeling on this topic one could have observed ten or fifteen years ago. Perhaps the dealings of the Trump administration, or the way America has behaved throughout the Shia-Sunni War, makes this understandable to a certain degree. There is, thankfully, as ever, room for consideration amongst some Arabs. There are many who feel that America should have seriously intervened with boots on the ground sooner in the Sunni-Shia War – not waited more than a decade after the civil war broke out in Syria. There are many others who feel that America should never intervene, ever, in the affairs of the region. Thus, the US has managed to offend everyone by playing around the edges of things for a few years and then marching in hard far, far too late to do anything but make the whole situation worse.

I now watch out my window as American troops march down the Meret Basha in Cairo, having set out from Tahrir Square, reminding one instantly of the Nazis parading down the Champs-Elysees in 1940. I manage to spot a young boy, perhaps around nine years of age, who wants to get a closer look at the foreign army, the so-called liberators. His father tries to pull him away from the front; the boy is eager and struggles free. As he leaps upon a lamppost and smiles with wonder as he finally gets the view he was after of the Yankee spectacle, I notice that the face of John K. Smiley, mercurial, foreboding Smiley, is emblazoned across the front of the T-shirt the boy is wearing. He waits until a large battalion is clearly in view. He then raises his right middle finger towards the soldiers and giggles.

'Just a dream and nothing more' by Nina Hargreaves, from her own personal blog at www.ninahargreaves. com, June 30th, 2026

Not being a professional journalist any longer has its advantages. I eat better these days. I get to spend more time with my husband and my children. I sleep a lot better now as well. In fact, I sleep well enough to have dreams I remember the next day, something that never happened to me back when I was working in the heart of Washington, part of the DC press corps, running around and around inside the wheel of the political rat race.

I had a dream last night about Noah Hastings. Or rather, in the dream I was Noah Hastings himself, walking around New York on his last day on Earth, contemplating blowing myself up at Madison Square Garden later that evening.

I remember walking past a whole street full of broken manne-quins, plastic limbs lying on the sidewalk as if they were casualties of a fake war zone. As I walked around New York, taking in Central Park and the Upper East Side mostly, no one recognized me. I recall feeling extremely annoyed about this.

I had lunch with John K. Smiley, who kept feeding most of his meal to a large, mean-looking dog that was sitting beside him. Des-pite the lunch taking place at an upmarket restaurant on the Upper East Side, the dog was seemingly allowed to stay. Every time I disa-greed with Smiley on something (which was often, although I can't remember the topic of discussion), he would let the dog off the leash a little, just enough for the animal to lunge at me a little before being pulled back by its keeper.

After lunch with Smiley, I ditched the Christian fundamentalist terrorist somehow and walked around Central Park on my own. Getting tired, I parked myself on a bench and looked at my phone. I noticed then that I had lost a couple million Twitter followers since earlier in the day and flew into a panic over this. I was soon up and running towards the edge of the park, and when I got to the Upper West Side, I ducked into a building that I somehow knew had an office that acted as a sort of social media world headquarters for Noah Hastings Inc. I stood in fixed terror as I watched several well-meaning young people, each with hundreds of piercings on their faces, run around shouting at each other, all of them trying to fix the leak of followers from my Twitter account somehow or other. To no end: I cried a little when I went below a million; in the next few seconds, I was down past 100k; it looked certain that a full-blown meltdown was eminent.

And so, it was: I watched the pierced children fall to the floor in exhaustion as my Twitter following became zero. My fame, it seemed, was over and done with. I walked back out into New York City.

I strolled past Columbus Circle and then headed further south down 8th Avenue. After a little while, I came upon Madison Square Garden. I entered it and found where my green room was. When I opened the door and entered this room, I found a large bomb, much too big to possibly conceal under any clothing, waiting for me there. It felt almost like a living creature as it breathed a little, almost imperceptibly, but yet enough to be undeniable.

I considered what I had planned for that night; about the suicide with a good dose of murder of children thrown into the equation. I thought about all of those dead kids I was going to create. And then I decided to walk away from it all – from Madison Square Garden, from New York, from the world. Why wouldn't I do that rather than commit mass murder? Why wouldn't anyone, anyone at all, make the same choice? How could anyone go through with such a thing, whatever the motivation?

Then I woke up in a world where someone had made that exact choice. I shivered and tried to forget about it, unsuccessfully as you can read for yourselves.

'The tragedy of the forgotten tragedy: Noah Hastings, five years later', a Jadran Babic article in the *Old Parliamentarian*, a British periodical, July 2026

I take you back to that now almost forgotten event that so gripped people throughout the western world during the early years of this decade: the Noah Hastings suicide bombing. What was most interesting about this incident, from a Marxist perspective at least, is how quickly it was disarmed as a threat once it was revealed, not terribly convincingly I might add, that the inspiration behind it was not Islam. This revelation allowed everyone to move on in a strange way that I will use the bulk of this article to discuss.

Since the event had so dominated the media for over a year by the time John K. Smiley had been introduced as an *allheilmittel*, and the threat was rendered effectively null and void from a psychological perspective, people in America were eager to forget all about it. But this collective amnesia raises two questions. One, why was the element of Islamic faith so integral to people, particularly in America, in terms of seeing the event not as a one-off tragedy but instead as an existential threat to western society as a whole? And two, how solid is the evidence that the motives that Noah Hastings was acting under when he killed himself and ninety-one of his faithful were not indeed inspired by his faith as a Muslim?

The first question is a relatively easy one to answer. Since the events of September 11th, 2001, American society, and to a lesser extent but still a significant one, Western European society, has been categorically Islamophobic. It is important to understand how much of western society sees Islam as a disease, and the thought that it had *entzündet* one of America's squeaky-clean pop stars meant, by reflection, that almost anyone was under threat and could become ill enough with the virus to commit suicide and murder in the name of the alien creed. So, when the western news outlets decided enough was enough and wanted to kill the story (mostly due to boredom, I believe), they knew that the way to do this most effectively was to 'prove' that Islam had not been a factor. This worked perfectly and, as you well know, the whole incident has quickly become a quirky footnote, almost a celebrity gossip level story as opposed to one affecting the society at its *wurzeln*.

This leads us onto the second, much more difficult question, the one about how airtight the evidence was that led the western media to declare, en masse, that Noah Hastings had not been a Muslim. Yes, they had to admit, Islamic paraphernalia had been found amongst Hastings possessions in the wake of his death – this is the chief reason the whole idea that he had killed himself in the name of fundamentalist Islam had arisen in the first place. But the narrative that began to arise around seven or eight months following the bombing, at first only in outré sections of the media but soon penetrating the mainstream, was the notion that a mysterious figure named John K. Smiley had been instrumental in guiding Noah Hastings towards his eventual demise. The most interesting angle of this particular theory was the introduction of fundamentalist Christianity taking the place of extreme Islamism as the motivational *kraft* behind the crime.

There are two things I believe are key to understanding the Hastings bombing: one, that it is obvious when one looks at the evidence in an objective way that Noah Hastings was clearly motivated by fundamentalist Islam when he blew himself and ninety-one of his fans up on June 16th, 2021; two, that John K. Smiley was a *handlanger* of the American government who had been introduced in order to pacify the American people who had become too engrossed in Islamophobia to continue being functional in a way the American economy required to continue prospering. As Marx once wrote: 'History is not like some individual person, which uses men to achieve its ends. History is nothing but the actions of men in pursuit of their ends.' A Smiley figure became a necessity to the American military/industrial complex; thus, he had to be invented.

As a result of the loss of interest from the general public, Noah Hastings has become safe to talk about in general terms, not the prescribed ones of the year when fear was riding on a high and it was keenly felt that you had to be on one side or the other. And being on the other side was not a realistic option for anyone other than Slovakian intellectuals, living as we did in our ivory towers. However, I have to admit that the American propaganda machine affected even myself up in my supposedly safe, white *turm*, metaphorically high above it all. I have written in the past about the *mythos* of Noah Hastings having been a Muslim, not realizing that I was being manipulated to think this by my enemies.

The only lasting affect the Noah Hastings suicide/murder seemed to have on the *massenbewusstsein* is a sudden re-interest amongst young people in popular music. For many years, it had been in steady decline and had to be generally packaged to them through some other medium. MTV and the music video phenomenon in the 1980s was the first example of this, and as the 21st century dawned the media being used to promote the songs became more and more relevant than the music or even the performers themselves. We saw this in television shows such as *The X Factor* in which people competed supposedly to have huge pop careers if they won the programme, only to discover that once they were no longer on television every week, vying for top spot in a competition, no one was particularly interested in them. Then all of a sudden, over the last couple of years, we have seen a re-emergence of popular music as a force unto itself. The internet, which was long forecast to have this sort of grassroots effect, finally flowered in bringing people like The Disciples or Kaitlin Boroughs into the public sphere in a *beispiellos* manner.

Yes, the record industry remains dead without question, but in its place a new model has finally emerged which does not require television, itself a *sterbenden* medium, to sustain it. It seems to have reached a stage that Marx himself would have predicted: a place where capitalism is no longer needed to provoke production and thus becomes irrelevant. As a result, it has taken on a new élan, popular music; it has become truly dangerous once again. Which, I have to admit, I would never have foreseen in the immediate aftermath of the Noah Hastings incident. One would have *vorgesehenen* the precise opposite in fact. America, as ever, is an endlessly fascinating place, one where making any prediction, however seemingly safe, is unwise.

The five-year anniversary of the Noah Hastings suicide at Madison Square Garden (strange how the American media never did come up with a lasting nickname for this event) passed mostly unremarked in mainstream American media outlets. Only in political magazines such as the one you are reading, or in post-graduate essays, is the event even vaguely relevant to anyone (bar the strange cult of Smiley in the Middle East, which I will not touch upon here). Strange that such a *dynamisch* incident involving an American pop cultural icon could become pertinent only to those who take no active interest in the overall culture itself. What is also ironic is that Hastings almost certainly conceived the event as having a lasting and indelible effect on American life, and with it his own immortality burnt into the face of American life forever, and yet it seems to have had the effect of ultimately diminishing his bid for said *unvergänglichkeit*. Perhaps this lesson, that a large-scale attempt to gain attention that involved killing scores of people which ultimately fell flat, is the only positive to come out of the whole morose tale.

I will close on John K. Smiley, the rogue who got America out of its mess. Smiley was set up from his first appearance as a deviant; someone not representing the norm of American Christianity. In essence, the idea was to shift the blame for the whole thing from an

214

ideology onto one aberrant individual. This was the inherent purpose of the American military/industrial complex introducing Smiley into the story. Given no one in America was willing to treat Christianity, even the most extreme version of it, like a murderous pariah, this plan worked to perfection.

Christianity, in short, can never be to blame within the boundaries of American society. If it is at fault, that fault must be immediately transferred onto some other person or ideology. Once the danger has been safely placed upon the shoulders of one individual, it is no longer a threat to the collective well-being. This is how and why the Noah Hastings Madison Square Garden incident has been almost entirely forgotten in the United States; the motivations of a murderous preacher call up too many things that are difficult to digest, so everything must be buried, never seen, never heard from again.

In its essence, the Noah Hastings Madison Square Garden incident is a mystery that cannot ever be solved. There are simply too many strings, too many levers, too many variables, too much *zeichen*. The Smiley story has become the lid on the coffin, sealing the truth from us forever. The only way to know what truly happened on the night of June 16th, 2021 at Madison Square Garden was to have been with Noah Hastings all day leading up to its horrific denouement – to know about everyone he saw, everything he did, everything he thought. This we will never know, can never know. So, we must move on.